Giuseppe Santarelli

LEGENDS
OF THE SIBILLINE
MOUNTAINS

Translated by Phoebe Leed and Nathan Neel

STAF
edizioni

© 2006 STAF edizioni
via XX settembre, 34
63021 AMANDOLA (AP)
staf.edizione@libero.it

ISBN 88-88532-07-2

STAF edizioni USA
79A Tremont St. #3
Cambridge MA 02139
staf.edizioni@gmail.com

INTRODUCTION

This pamphlet, on the legends of the Sibilline Mountains, was born from a double feeling of affection: one for the sanctuary of the Madonna dell'Ambro, and the other for the land of Piceno, sweet cradle of my birth.

The Sanctuary dell'Ambro is particularly dear to me, to the faithful of Piceno, to the Capuchin fathers of the Marches who have officiated there for decades with moving dedication, and to all those who harbor a secret devotion to Mary, mother of Jesus.

As the Phlegraean Fields, the cave of the Cumaean Sibyl, and Lake Avernus were to classical antiquity, so the Sibilline Mountains, the grotto of the Sibyl, and the Lake of Pilate were to the late Middle Ages and early Renaissance. The Sanctuary dell'Ambro was set amongst the Sibilline Mountains as if to disperse the demonic shadows which stain the dark traditions of the grotto and the lake. Bartolo Longo wrote, in a supplication to the Madonna of Pompci, that in pagan times unbridled idolatry predominated there; in modern times the Virgin of the Rosary rules. The same could be written of the Madonna dell'Ambro in reference to the Sibilline Mountains, a place which in a very remote past

was an   alarming temple of sorcery, an obligatory school for necromancers and shady tricksters.

Then there is the affection for the Picenean soil. Taking advantage
of two celebrated verses of Dante and stretching the meaning, I venture
to say:

> *Since love of my native place constrained me,*
> *I gathered up the scattered leaves*
>
> *(Inferno XIV 1-2)*
> *Trans. John D. Sinclair*

Everyone has a great " love of my native place," especially if it is
the treasure chest of delightful childhood memories. The active desire
is aroused to know the glorious and hopefully the inglorious events,
and if possible, to collect them. To "gather" the varied and dispersed
memories like "scattered leaves" and to make of them a small but
homogenous anthology, thereby offering reading matter even to those
who do not have much sympathy or, perhaps, adequate preparation, for
difficult philological and historical studies.

If those memories are fairytales, which light up the tender imagi-
nations of our infancy, then they exert on the soul a seductive and perpetual fascination. Consequently, the desire is whetted to revive them
concretely, to be enjoyed by oneself and others.

The Sibilline Mountains were the majestic and immaculate setting
of my infancy, spent in a Picenean hamlet, Montegiberto, small and
pretty like a candy box floating at the summit of an emerald green hill,
between the mountains and the sea, with its buildings of red terra cotta
in the sober design of the urban seventeenth century, admirable for its
prosperity and intimacy.

From there I, small and heedless, would contemplate those mountains. They looked to me like bluish glass, which is how the central hills
of the Marches appeared by virtue of a unique atmospheric refraction.

Indeed Leopardi, who admired them from an analogous geographic position a little bit to the north, was deeply affected. In his supreme verse he refers to the "blue mountains":

What sweet dreams were inspired in me by the sight
Of that distant sea, those blue mountains,
Which I discovered there, and which I thought to cross one day
Imagining mysterious worlds, mysterious
Happiness for my life.

(Le Ricordanze vs 21:24)

"Mysterious worlds and mysterious mountains," in which enchanted legends of unusual fascination are hidden.

When, still a babbling child, I asked mama if those mountains were really made of "glass," she told me yes. She added that up there, in a golden palace, a queen lives, dressed all in gold, with long golden hair, who weaves and weaves an endless golden cloth, who weaves and weaves night and day and that the melodious hissing of her shuttle and the harmonious strokes of her loom can be heard by putting an ear to the mouth of a grotto. "Cupa,cupa," coming from who knows where...

It was the beautiful legend of the Sibyl avalanching from the grotto down the precipices, into the river valleys of the Tenna, of the lively Ete, and of the Aso, and from there it ricochets, after a hundred metamorphoses, to the happy hills with the lightness of an angel's wing, to lose itself finally down there in the infinite blue of the Adriatic Sea....because infinity is the natural landing place of all genuine fables.

This gilded legend had been sleeping for years in the prehistory of my infantile memory, and was reawakened in all its fascination one autumn afternoon when I visited the "Infernaccio" with some friends.

Sudden astonishment left me breathless!

3

The "Infernaccio," a terrifying name for a magical cleft of mountain, is at the source of the Tenna River, which at this point is as impetuous as an untamed colt. Tumultuous and frothing, it has carved the rock, in an intense activity of millions of years, patiently, according to the method of "gutta cavat lapidem" (a drop hollows out stone). And it goes on working, indefatigable and imperturbable.

Hell as pictured in the fervid fantasies of medieval men would have to be just like this. Just like the "Infernaccio," made of fearsome ravines, cut in the dark and weeping rock, where a ray of sun barely filters down to roll like a glittering diamond on the dark watery mirror of the torrent.

The "Pisciarelle" is the vestibule of the "Infernaccio." It consists of an enormous boulder, jutting out high above, from which drizzles a cloth of watery threads, with the characteristic symphony of a torrential rain, of a pelting shower. These are the copious tears of a wounded and irritable mountain.

Crossing a little wooden bridge, which trembles with the restless waves of the river, the path enters a cleft in the rock. Looking upwards brings on a nervous shudder, the sensation of sliding inadvertently to the bottom of a very high cliff.

Further along, the steep slope of the pathway cut in the rock climbs into the heart of the "Infernaccio," a realm of darkness and dampness. There is a deep cavern, where threads of light never penetrate, or, in a happier hypothesis, where light penetrates obliquely, as if to reassure the visitor that he is still on Earth and not really in Hell. Meanwhile the heavy torrent, like a large watchdog, howls at the bottom and keeps the boldest at a distance.

Like Dante leaving the Inferno, one goes from a "natural dungeon" to "seeing the stars," but always with the two narrow walls of iron colored rock looming overhead. On the right side, the boughs of the pines hang green in front of the pale vein of rock, which continues along the edge on the opposite side.

Further along, the path runs through a wood, no longer pines, straight to the ancient hermitage of San Leonardo, which the kind diligence of a Capuchin father is now bringing back to its ancient splendor.

That autumn afternoon, the wood seemed enchanted: the leaves rustled with every breath of air and scattered the rays of the sun into a thousand fringes of gold. From the ridge a panorama spread out as far as the eye could see, all the way to the sea. Behind, to the southwest, the crown of the Monte della Sibilla loomed, sheltering, majestic, and menacing.

Up there the magical legends were in flower. Memories returned with a new intensity, with a voluptuousness of recollection not tasted since times long past, vividly reanimated. The desire was born to define them better through a speedy inquiry.

And from this desire, like fruit from flowers, these humble pages came to light. Above all these pages are meant to recall to the readers of today those ancient legends, germinated in a cultural soil and from a fertile popular imagination which honors our land and our ancestors, obedient to the beautiful poetics of the fairytales which gladdened the hours spent at the hearth during the long evenings of winter.

The intention here is neither to sully the native freshness of these fairy tales, nor to disregard the surprising literary and philological flowering which concerns them. These are pages that run at the same time on the light wing of the imagination and on the austere footprints of erudition, wishing to please both the reader eager to amuse himself with the fables and the reader greedy for cultural facts. Perhaps both will be dissatisfied with this hybrid. However that might be, this is not an exhaustive investigation, but only a quick summary of facts and problems already explored by authoritative masters and related here in the tone of a simple tale.

*   *   *   *

This edition, with respect to the first, has been enlarged, in the text as well as in the notes, with a number of appropriate additions. In the text, the fabric of the philological discussion and the evocation of the fable has been thickened with citations from new authors, with references from more scholars, with more precise definitions of some problems, and with the presentation of new documents. By these means the resulting book should be richer and better articulated.

The additions to the notes are ample because it was preferable to reproduce, literally or in summary, both the ancient documents, precious for our legends, and the passages of the scholars and philologists. These develop the text and scholars can not only find basic bibliographical information but also whole passages of analysis.

Hence the discussion of the text finds a constant and explicit confirmation in the notes, notwithstanding the personal reconstruction of the legends and of the philological problems. Hopefully this will not extinguish the secret flame of the Sibilline fables!

CHAPTER I

THE QUEEN SIBYL AND HER ENCHANTED GROTTO

Piovane writes that the Sibilline Mountains probably remain "the most legendary of central Italy," and it's true.

Perhaps the same harshness of these mountains, scoured by the whistling wind, devoured by precipitous torrents, and drilled by peculiar karst phenomena, has contributed not a little to furthering a series of witch legends and making this place celebrated in the 14th and 15th centuries throughout all Europe for magical fairytales and necromantic initiations. The "infernal" and "funereal" names of certain places seems to confirm it; Devil's Peak, Grotto of the Devil, Pit of Hell, Infernaccio, Valley of Hell, Dark Valley, Mountain of the Dead, Bad Passage, Witches Pass ...
It's enough to make your skin crawl!

* * *

There are two nuclei of the Sibilline Mountain legends, two places where they germinated as if by a magic spell. One nucleus refers to the Grotta della Sibilla (Grotto of the Sibyl) and the other to the Lago di Pilato (Lake of Pilate).
The two legendary places have in common, at least apparently, only the ingredient of magic, in so far as the stories and the characters which populate them are quite distinct, with unmistakable fantastical-literary resolutions. The lake, in fact, lives in a dark necromantic atmosphere in the tragic remembrance of Pontius Pilate; the grotto, on the other hand, trembles in the bewitching light of an enchanted realm bearing the memory of a seductive Sibyl.
Here we will speak first of the Grotta della Sibilla and then the Lago di Pilato.

Why the Grotto of the Sibyl? Did the cult of some pagan divinity prosper up there in italo-roman antiquity?

Some, like the learned Gaston Paris, Pio Rajna, Fernand Desonay, Giovanni Crocioni, Febi Allevi, etc., pursued this idea, raising above all the name of the Goddess Cybele, without arriving, however, at a definitive hypothesis. Paolucci denies their theory, defining the Appenine Sibyl as "a product of the popular imagination without any historical link whatsoever." (1) But of this we will talk later.

In fact, around the end of the 14th century and the beginning of the 15th century, the Grotta della Sibilla began to be spoken of as an enchanted magical place and the mysterious abode of a queen, Alcina or Sibilla or Venus as she might be called.

Fabbi, following Fumi's lead, thought that at the time of the Avignon exile of the papal court the resurgence of superstitions and heresies in the Papal States could have favored the expansion, or even the creation, of the unique myth of the Sibyl. (2)

According to Pabst — who describes the Italy of the 14-15th centuries as a land of temptation for the knights from beyond the Alps — the beginning of the legend might coincide with the literary creation of *Guerin Meschino* by Andrea da Barberino (circa 1410). Barberino brought his hero to these solitary mountains because of their noted salubrious waters, dear to necromancers. (3)

But maybe the legend of the Sibyl came earlier, because it is improbable that an author would, out of the blue, create a magic place without a preexisting popular stimulus. Several writers from the 14th century on speak of a transmigration of the Virgilian Sibyl from the cave of Cumae to the grotto of the Sibillines, coinciding with the advent of Christianity. Lalli of Norcia, a poet of the 16th century, writes in his *Tito Vespasiano overo Gerusalemme Desolata:*

It is rumored that from Cumae, where the first
rooms the illustrious prophetess obtained,
while over there with too frequent oppression
of her quiet, she had to leave
In the remote inaccessible summit
of the Norcian mountain she came to repose
From the curious people there she hides
and high secrets rarely to others reveals.
(canto II, stanza XII) (4)

The fable goes that the Sibyl was exiled to a dreadful spot in the Sibillines, veritably at the mouth of Hell, and that she would be unable to die before the end of the world.

But what physical and moral characteristics have been attributed to her? Here—as Paolucci explains—it is necessary to distinguish two groups of authors. For some authors, especially Italians, (Trissino, Lalli, etc.), the Sibyl, even fallen from her pedestal—after the triumph of Christianity, which wouldn't tolerate the cult of false pagan myths— remains a dignified and beautiful woman. Trissino depicts her in this way in his *L'Italia Liberata dai Goti*:

Most ancient of years and wisdom;
that which thanks to her heaven grants
One can know all human things
What is, what was, and what must come.
(Book XXIV) (5)

In sum, she is the ancient Sibyl of Virgil, operating from a different abode, more inaccessible and more mysterious.

For other authors, however, above all the Germans and French, the Sibyl is a Circe enchantress, in partnership with the devil to ensnare in her net knights in search of adventure and love. She is a charmer expert in the magical arts, with a sparkling palace saturated with lust. For good reason she is linked with the classical Venus or Ariosto's Alcina. Thus the Monte della Sibilla is also identified by some with *Venusberg* (Mountain of Venus) in the myth of Tannhäuser. The infiltration of components of the chivalric European literature, with markings of the Arthurian cycle, seems to run suggestively through the plot of the legend of the Sibyl.

Paolucci talks intelligently about the transformation of the Sibyl from wise prophetess to bewitching seductress, pointing out first of all the "substantial difference" between the theme of voluptuousness and that of prophecy in the figure of the Appenine Sibyl. He differentiates the group of Italian writers (Trissino, Lalli, Mecchi, etc.), inclined to view the mysterious personage in the garb of an uncontaminated soothsayer, from the group of German and French writers, who, ignorant of such an aspect, highlighted her role of voluptuous seductress in accordance with the well known motif "of the enchantress and the adventurous knight."

From this perspective the Italian writers spontaneously tie together the tradition of the Cumaen Sibyl and the tradition of the Appenine Sibyl. In addition there was also the analogy of places (grotto-lake) and the diffusion of the Virgilian legend in the Middle Ages.

The transformation occurs for the first time in *Guerin Meschino* by Andrea da Barbarino, in which the Sibyl lives in the double dimension of prophetess and seductress.

According to Paolucci (who examines the subject in depth), "between the soothsayer of the primitive Appenine tradition, and the Venus that the German visitors dreamed of, was the fairy Sibyl, identified in the popular imagination with Morgana and Alcina." (6)

The Enchanted Grotto

The grotto sits about 2,175 meters high on the Monte della Sibilla. To describe it, not geographically but "literarily," would require a diligent study linking together all the authors who have written about it, from Andrea Barberino to Antoine De La Sale, to Hemmerlin, to Alberti, to Ortoel, etc.

Here we will describe the salient aspects held by all of these authors, drawing particularly from the celebrated little work of A. De La Sale, *Le Paradis de la Reine Sibylle*. (7)   His description, compared for example to Andrea Da Barberino's total fantasy, appears to be factual, thanks to his experiences with the Sibilline mountain people.

A. De La Sale wrote about his own ascent to the grotto, guided by a local doctor, a certain Giovanni Da Sora, and by some inhabitants of Montemonaco. He wanted to give an account of these melancholy places, wrapped in darkly sensual legends (legends to which he personally didn't give any credence). He described his excursion to the Sibillines, in May 1420, with its fabulous events involving certain knights and curious people, to the princess of Borgogna, Agnese di Borbone, sister of Phillip the Good and wife of Charles 1 of Borbone.

But a suspicion could arise—did he go all the way up to the very top, to the highest altitude, the adventurous Antoine, or was it rather a work of imagination? His description of these places, at times of a surprising precision, should give flight to any scepticism. After all, Petrarch, climbing Mt Ventoso many years earlier, offered a suggestive lesson in Alpinism to all readers with agile legs.

De La Sale recounts the facts based on his excursion and on the testimony of two young men of Montemonaco, whom he had questioned. They, together with another three youths, had descended into the bowels of the grotto, while Antoine himself had stopped at its threshold.

The grotto had a narrow gothic entrance, in the form of a shield. A boulder obstructed the passageway, necessitating a descent on all fours into the interior Immediately to the right of the narrow opening one encountered a square room carved into the rock, through which a few rays of light filtercd. To continuc onc must thrcad oneself through a narrow perpendicular tunnel, which runs steeply into the heart of the rock, down, down, always further down.

Antoine did not continue beyond the square room, perhaps because he feared for his life, perhaps because he didn't want the others to believe he was a reckless knight, in love with infernal adventures. However, in a previous expedition the five young men of Montemonaco, equipped with long ropes, torches, flints, and foodstuffs for five days, had gone further.

What a chilling experience! The tunnel descended for about three miles, then lengthened into an ample corridor. There was a tomblike silence, and dense darkness broken only by the flickering torches casting on the walls horrible and gigantic figures, which trembled at every step. At one point, a violent wind erupted from a fissure that split the cavern. The five youths were not willing to take a step further; they risked being carried off like twigs by the whirlwind. The howling deafened them, the tempestuous gusts repulsed and froze them. Abandoning everything, they beat a horror-struck retreat with their hearts in their mouths.

But other curious people were willing to go beyond the outlet of the wind. De La Sale relates that Antonio Fumato, a priest of Montemonaco, subject to easy hallucinations, refers to having accompanied two Germans to the grotto, much further in than the vein of wind, as far as two metal doors. According to the priest's account, the wind stops after fifteen "tese" (a "tese" corresponds to 1.949 meters).

Whoever has the courage to enter the whirlwind and to advance a few steps, then, is easily capable of going further along the way. After a descent of three "tese" more, there is a bridge made of a mysterious substance, very long and no wider that a foot. In sum, one of many "devil's bridges" encountered in the adventures of medieval knights. One legendary bridge consisted of a long razor's edge; as a test the hero had to cross it hanging in space, slicing his hands with each bound, until reaching the opposite side.

Under the bridge opens a bottomless abyss. A thundering river courses through it and every jolting vibration causes fear of a sudden collapse of the rock pillars. But here is the magical charm. With the first step onto the bridge, it gets wider and wider; the abyss grows smaller, the roaring of the river progressively diminishes. And on the other side the grotto squares itself into a plateau which resembles a phantasmagoric tunnel, traversed by a spacious and delightful street. At the end of this are two dragons, one in front of the other, sculpted in a sparkling material, animated in their magical shapes but immobile in their supreme solemnity. Their eyes are luminous beacons which illuminate everything around.

Beyond the two dragons a narrow corridor opens, about a hundred steps long, leading to a quadrangular open space. Here are the two metal doors which beat violently one against the other, so that they would crush those who wished to pass.

It was these doors—the priest of Montemonaco told De La Sale—which terrified the Germans. Nevertheless, after a first moment of being at a loss, they rashly tried to pass through. And in this they succeeded. But the priest, who had not wanted to go further, waited for them in vain for a long time.

The German Knight

Antoine heard reports of the other parts of the grotto from the living voices of the inhabitants of Montemonaco, who told of the impossible exploits of a German knight and his groom who penetrated into the mysterious realm of the Sibyl. These two could be the same Germans described by the priest Antonio Fumato.

The knight came from Germany in the company of his faithful groom, determined to fathom the mystery of the grotto. On his return from his fantastic journey into the bowels of the cave, he related that beyond the metal doors was a sumptuous and luminous door, and that the grotto glittered with a thousand lights reflected from the glimmer of torches, as if it was made of crystal. Silence ruled, until the two Germans heard voices which they lost on the mysterious wings of an echo. Becoming thoughtful, they began to be afraid. Suddenly a fascinating voice reached them and asked them questions. On the reply of the knight the door opened and a glittering queen, with a festive multitude of sweet damsels and youths, welcomed them amidst the shining glory of dress and jewels.

It was the Paradise of the Sibyl, with the blooming flowers of youthful beauty, lovelier than a dream, overflowing with riches grander than desire itself. The queen showered the German knight with exquisite kindness and took him through sparkling rooms, amongst the glow of gilded alcoves and iridescent furniture, surrounded by the crowd of gay and carefree youth.

Those who lived in the grotto were able to speak all the languages of the world after being there a mere three hundred days, and after only nine days they could understand all of them. But the wonder didn't end there. All the inhabitants of this paradisaical realm remained in the grotto, alive, until the end of time! And then? The queen answered: that which was agreed upon will be fulfilled; that is enough.

And her majesty the Sibyl explained to the knight and his groom that they could leave after the 8th day, or after the 30th, or if they still had not gone, after the 330th. If even then they weren't willing to leave, they must understand that according to the law of her realm, they wouldn't be allowed to return to the world.

A stunning maiden, chosen from the most beautiful of the realm, gladdened the exhilarating sojourn of the knight. Another woman lovely beyond imagination was chosen for his groom.

But from time to time the sting of conscience made itself felt in the soul of the knight; he was dedicating himself to a life of inexhaustible lust, in the service of the devil; he would forget his Lord, who was crucified for his salvation.

The Germans knew they were in the company of the devil, when at midnight of every Friday they were abandoned by their lovers, who left them to go to the queen along with all the other irresistible women of the realm. And all these ladies—horrors!!!—transformed themselves into disgusting snakes, staying like that until midnight Saturday. Afterwards they returned more splendid than ever to their erstwhile lovers, always young because old age was banned and pain did not have the right of citizenship, because there one did not suffer heat or cold, but enjoyed only the full sum of delight.

Nevertheless at the expiration of the 330th day the knight wanted to leave the fabulous court of the Sibyl, in order not to run the risk of eternal damnation. But the groom, who floated in pleasures ever more unimaginable, put up resistance. After enormous effort he decided to follow his master only because of the loyalty and the affection he bore him.

The knight took off the garments glowing with rubies, assumed the moment he entered into this world of fairytales, and put back on the garments of a German knight. A procession accompanied them as far as the metal doors. At the moment of leave-taking the tears of the women made the two hesitate and brought them to the point of renouncing their departure. But with an effort of will...away they went with torches lit, towards the light of the sun!

All the difficulties of the inward journey, namely, the crashing doors, the dragons, the narrow bridge, the blast of wind, had vanished as if by a spell. Only by enchantment did they appear to those who made their way towards the grotto, and were fatal on the return only for those who had remained in the court of the Sibyl for more than 330 days.

The knight, along with his servant, made his way to the vault of Rome to implore the Pope's pardon, heartbroken with remorse. Outwardly the Pope was hard on him; he resolutely withheld absolution for sins so serious, though in his heart he only wanted to give the sinner a beneficial warning. But the knight, tortured and inconsolable, despairing of the salvation of his soul, retraced his steps.

After delivering letters to various pastors of the Sibilline Mountains, he was swallowed up forever in the grotto of the Sibyl. One of the letters reads that whoever desires news of the knight to whom the pope had denied pardon, should know that he could be found in the paradise of the Sibyl.

Together, naturally, with his groom, to whom the paradise was very pleasing, more so than the absolution of the Pope!

And here "the brief tale is finished."

Alberti, about a century and a half after De La Sale, offers a description of the realm of the Sibyl no less fantastic and certainly more bloodcurdling. The "mad fable" (as he calls it) speaks of "grand and magnificent palaces inhabited by many people". The lovers get together only by day because at night "the men as well as the women become frightening serpents, along with the Sibyl" and all of those who want to enter here have to "take lascivious pleasures with the aforementioned sickening serpents." For those who return from that fantastic world the Sibyl reserves on earth "graces and privileges" by means of which they pass "their days happily." (8)

Rather insignificant details about the structure and more significant ones about life in the realm of the Sibyl can be found in the pages that follow, both in the descriptions given by the people who visited it and in the survey of the scholars who spoke of it.

Clearly the charms of the European chivalric literature, with all its diabolical and infernal fairy tales, with enchantments and sorcery in profusion, have substantially influenced the formation of our fable. It is also clear that the popular fantasy, inexhaustible mine for the creation and elaboration of myths and legends, has impressed its vital signs on it. As De La Sale writes, he drew constantly on the voice of the people of Montemonaco for stories about the Sibyl, while determining that their accounts were totally invented and impossible to believe.

But of course! Who would want to believe in the realm of the Sibyl?

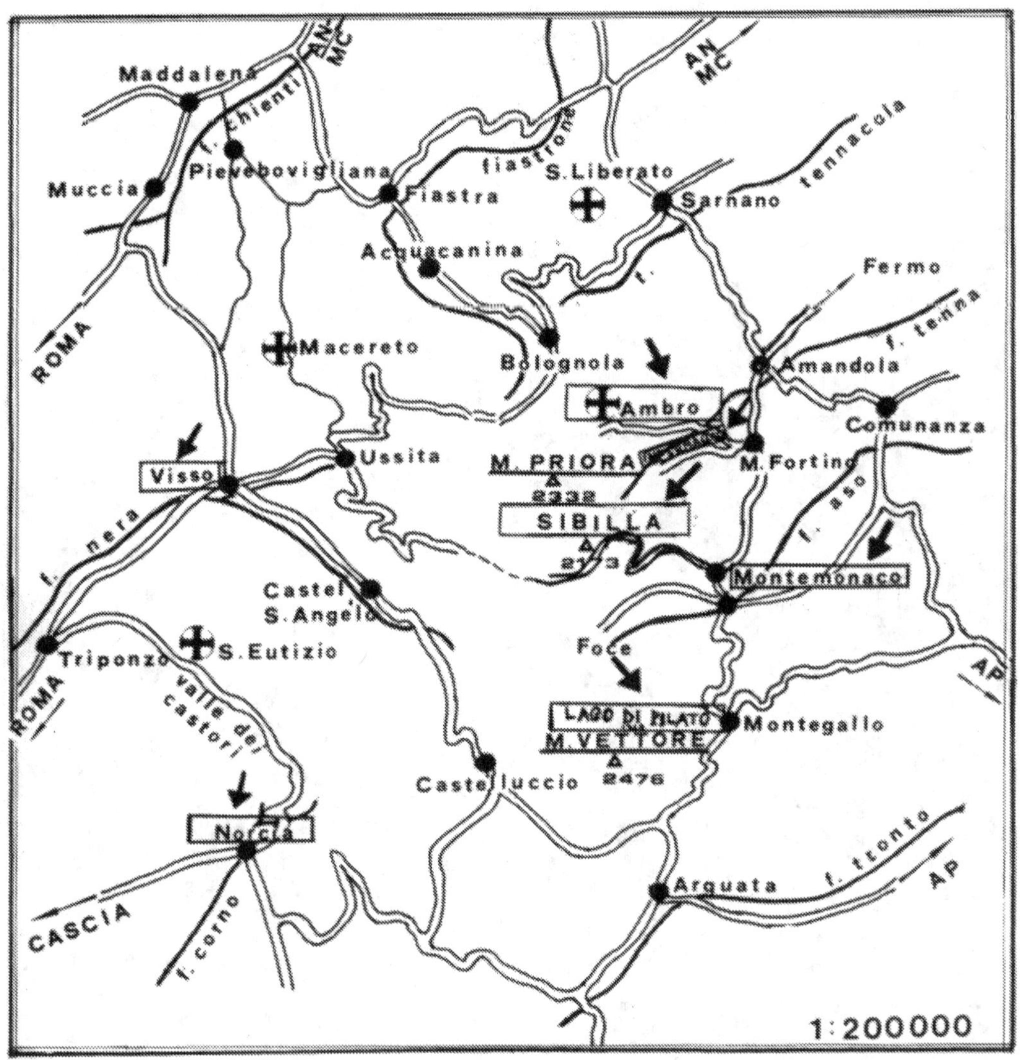

The Sibilline Region, where the magical legends flourish. The places of major interest in the Sibilline myths and those mentioned with particular attention in this book are indicated with an arrow.

19

The Sanctuary of the Madonna of the Ambro, set almost in the heart of the Sibilline Mountains, between Mt Manardo and Mt. Priora (on the left in the photo). Site of an ancient Marian cult, already marked on a parchment of 1073, it is today a lively center of religious life and the goal for many pilgrims. In recent times it has also become a compulsory stop and reference point for tourists and for lovers of the natural beauty and the fascinating legends of the Sibillines.

The legendary places of the Sibillines in a drawing by A. De La Sale following his excursion of 1420. Note that here the Lago di Pilato is marked as "Lac de la Sibille" and the river Aso as "Asno". One can clearly make out Montemonaco, the principlebase of his excursion. The valuable drawing is kept at the National Library of Paris (Reserve des Imprimes, Z. 355).

The Lago di Pilato with its double mirror of water and the little island in the middle. It was the destination, in past centuries, of necromancers who climbed up here to consecrate the "book of commands".

The Monte della Sibilla (Mountain of the Sibyl) with its famous crown, seen from Montemonaco, base for ancient and modern visitors to the grotto. The palace of the bewitching and all foreseeing Sibyl was imagined to be up there.

22

CHAPTER II

THE DEMONIACAL LAGO DI PILATO

The mythification of the miniscule Lago di Pilato/Lake of Pilate is every bit as fascinating. Hoisted up on a high western ridge of Mt. Vettore, it stretches out in the form of two lenses, like the glasses of a rattlesnake. Under a dark stormy sky it turns a sinister red, as frightening flashes of lightening zig-zag and thunderclaps tumble amongst grim clouds. (9)

The legend of the lake, according to literary documents, is older than that of the grotto. In the beginning, however, the story didn't refer to Pilate, but rather to a mirror lake frequented by the devil and his fatal followers. The first to describe the lake was the Benedictine Pierre Bersuire in his *Reductium Morale* (book xiv, chapter 30) around the second half of the 1300's. Studied and published in part by Graf in his notable essay about our lake (10), the legend of Pilate is not mentioned there. It is recorded instead by Fazio degli Uberti around 1360, in his *Dittamondo*, which speaks of Mt. Pilate and not of the lake. In terms of tradition, the infiltration of Franco-German imports and the famous Lucerne mountain with its own Lago di Pilato must be bourne in mind.

The Legend of Pilate

But how does Pilate get mixed up in the Sibilline Mountains?

The unfortunate Roman governor, who with a bowl of water deluded himself that he had washed his hands of Christ's blood, was thrown to the vengeance of the imagination of the Christian populace. He was hounded through all the countries of Europe, and in the end swallowed up in our infernal mountains.

The legends about the end of Pilate are numerous and all are bloodcurdling. In his famous *Annali Ecclesiastici*, Baronio, drawing from Eusebio, Cassiodoro and others, was disposed to accept the thesis of the death of the Roman proconsul at Vienne, and was convinced that Pilate killed himself in a moment of supreme desperation. (11)

Graf gives various versions of the death of Pontius Pilate, one of which bleeds drops of vindictive rancor. It goes: Pilate was sewn up in a sack of hide–such as was used for parricides–together with a rooster, a viper, and a monkey, and was then left to roast in the sun with this company of beasts.

Another fable says that Pilate, while in Rome, plunged into a whirlpool which opened up suddenly at his feet. Another more widespread legend elaborates that the unfortunate one wasn't at peace even after he was killed. His corpse, thrown first into the Tiber, passed from land to land, carrying everywhere ruin and misfortune like a wandering curse. The corpse appeared amongst the waves of the Rhone; going upstream toward the source, it ended up in the Alps, always in horrible places, in wells or lakes.

For good reason there exists another lake of Pilate in Switzerland–as has been mentioned. Hemmerlin speaks of it towards the middle of the 1400's, recollecting fantastically the marvelous atmospheric phenomena.

Nevertheless, the Pilate of our lake has a precise legend, all his own. And again Antoine De La Sale relates it with suggestive and astounding details.

According to Antoine, the local people said that Tito Vespasian, after the destruction of Jerusalem, brought Pilate with him to Rome, where he was publicly executed. The chronological error of popular hearsay did not escape De La Sale and he discourses at length on how Pilate was instead alive and was punished in the time of Tiberio. However it was, these people said that Pilate, before dying, asked the emperor for a favor— that his corpse would be put in a cart drawn by buffalos, and left to the power of fate. The emperor obliged but ordered some of his envoys to follow the cart on its whole adventurous course.

The buffalos, panting, finally reached the Sibilline Mountains. Here they plunged headlong into the reddened waves of our lake with the body of Pilate, which disappeared forever into its aquatic bowels.

Even the geographical aspects of the mountain of the lake, according to the narration of Antoine, have fable-like tints. The summit is 10 miles high; from there the sea at both Rome and Venice can be seen. The harshness of the ground is such that not even the shadow of a tuft of green can take root there. The lake doesn't have a bottom, and yet in the middle an enchanted little island rises, favorite destination of the necromancers. From there gushes a subterranean spring which comes to light at Foce and gives life to the Aso River, fraught with thousands of perils for man and beast.

How different the Mountain of the Lake is from the nearby Mountain of the Sibyl, the top of which—always according to De La Sale—is strewn with thousands of nameless flowers, rare and perfumed! Even today it is like that!

To be sure, in the heart of the Monte della Sibilla a "paradise" opens up. Even if it's only an infernal illusion, it is still a "paradise," while in the Lago di Pilato the king of darkness, with his necromantic friends, stirs sinisterly.

The Lake—Goal of Necromancers

By the time that Pierre Bersuire provided the first reports of the lake, it was already known that a sulfurous demonic atmosphere prevailed here. Pierre, who assures us he has obtained the facts from a "prelate most gracious of faith," writes that the lake had been consecrated since ancient times to the devils who live here in visible forms. No one can come near—excepting necromancers—without falling into their deadly clutches; an encircling wall has been built around it which not even the necromancers can breach. Then there is the bloodcurdling knowledge that the city of Norcia, in order to avoid being destroyed by storms, every year must choose one of their inhabitants and throw him in offering to the ravenous demons of the lake, who immediately tear him to pieces.(12)

Classical and medieval memories circulate in this narrative, like the myth of the Minotaur–there the Athenians were obligated to offer in sacrifice seven

girls and seven boys every nine years—or like the Dantesque description of
the pit of hell, used by Malebranche.

This demonic and tragic character of the lake is encountered again in De
La Sale. He relates how a priest, surprised up there by some mountain people during their necromantic exercises, was taken to Norcia and there tortured
and burned alive. Another, for the same reason, was cut into pieces and
thrown into the lake, turning it ever more the color of blood.

Arnolfo di Harff tells us that on the path to the lake there were gallows,
a rather tragic admonishment to the bold sorcerers that tried to hide there.
Woe unto those the authorities caught at the lake; the gallows were all ready
for an immediate hanging!

In the popular imagination, the infernal tenants of the lake end up by
transforming themselves into fish—while the soft girls of the grotto trans-
mute themselves into serpents. Such squalid metamorphoses are also
described by Trissino in *L'Italia Liberata Dai Goti* and before him the
humanist Flavio Biondo records the same—without believing in it.

The Rite of the Necromancers

Graf mentions a sermon in Latin by Fra Bernardino Bonavoglia da
Foligno, who lived in the 15th century. It relates the unsettling ceremonies
conducted by necromancers at the Lago di Pilato. (13)

As soon as the necromancer, whether from a country near or far, reaches
the lake, he forms three concentric circles. Placing himself in the middle of
the third with some offerings destined for the malign spirits, he calls the
desired demon by name, reading the magic book which he wants to consecrate. An infernal clamor follows which becomes a voice and says:

"Why do you call me?"

And the sorcerer answers, "I want to consecrate this book to you and I want
you to pledge to execute everything that is contained herein, every time I request
it of you. Do you want to know the price? I give you my soul in payment!"

So then the devil seizes the book, tracing over it mysterious signs and pledging to carry out every type of evil when it is read by the sorcerer.

An irrevocable pact, for eternity.

Virgil (who in medieval times was considered a sorcerer) was said to have etched one of these magic circles, as well as Cecco D'Ascoli. (14)

According to Fra Bernardino da Foligno, a necromancer once invoked the name of a certain devil at the lake. The answer came from the water, between strangled gurglings, that this "farfarello" had gone to Ascoli Piceno, pledging to put to the sword various exiles and hooligans of the city. Descending immediately to Ascoli Piceno, the sorcerer learned from a holy Franciscan brother that the previous night thirty exiles had been hung and that many citizens of the two opposing factions had butchered each other.

Needless to say, according to the preacher the sorcerer renounced his diabolical exercises for ever. The amateurs and the professionals of the magical arts, who climb up in swarms to the Lago di Pilato, should be discouraged, be they astrologers intent on deciphering the hieroglyphics of their books in order to predict the future, or wizards in search of new infernal recipes for their enchantments, or sorcerers, or witches, or magicians; in sum, those devoted body and soul to the spirit of evil.

CHAPTER III

OTHER LEGENDS

Other legends, although they don't flow together organically in the literature, run through the gorges of the Sibilline Mountains, rolling from mouth to mouth amongst the imaginative mountaineers of the two mountain sides. They are of a pleasing immediacy, thanks to their gaudy inconsistencies, logical and chronological, which are two of the deepest ingredients of the fable.

Up until a few years ago, the people still sang:

> *E me ne vojo gi tanto lontano*
> *Du che fa guera lo Guerin Meschino*
> *Du sta l'amore mio per capitano.* (15)

> And I want to go far away
> Where Guerin Meschino fights
> There is my love, who rules me

Ansano Fabbi refers to a remote popular tradition regarding the origins of the grotto of the Sibyl. In the 8th century a.d. a devil took up residence in the cave and, assuming the appearance of a bewitching goddess, gave answers like an ancient Sibyl. She was of a unique beauty, and those who dared to venture into the grotto never left it again; they were swallowed by the infernal labyrinth in a fatal game of sorcery. Giovanni, the Bishop of Norcia, together with the monks of St. Eutizio, proclaimed three days of strict fasting and performed potent exorcisms against the spirit of evil. It was then possible for some bold souls to explore the grotto with impunity. And horrors! They discovered human skeletons, the macabre remains of those who dreamed of a splendid reign of voluptuousness; and an inscription which warned severely; "Fideles fugite ab hac peste"; which means, "Faithful, flee from this plague."(16)

But they didn't flee. It was said that Cecco d'Ascoli, again before the written legend had fully gelled, climbed these mountains to the Lago di Pilato to consecrate his book of commands. Armed with some infernal device, he succeeded in draining a salubrious spring in the neighborhood of Ussita, "the water of the Bath at the head of Vallazza, good and holy and miracle-working, at least so it was said it was, before Cecco d'Ascoli suffocated it."(17)

The Ascolane astrologer infuriated the inhabitants of the place for at least two centuries. In 1468 there were still those who remembered, like the Ussitano whose archaic words are quoted above.

But, especially in the 1400s, the Sibilline districts of Ussita were particularly happy places for the sorcerers, until the local authorities intervened with severe penalties against "certain enchanters dressed as monks, who roamed around the valleys 'incantando et extorlocando' (enchanting and extorting) and saying they wanted to discover a treasure hidden under the earth by means of magical and diabolical arts." (18)

Cecco d'Ascoli, who in the opinion of the populace was more endowed with magical powers than poetic ones, may have completed another marvelous spell when in one night he called into existence a magnificent stone bridge. A "bridge of the devil," yes, but still a bridge!

So the demonic effects of the cave and the lake reached down into the valleys. Moreover, the spirits that lived up there descended as far as Pretare in the sweetest form of sparkling fairies, greedy to dance with the prettiest youth of the village. Up until a few years ago some elders of the place swore to having seen them and, who knows, to have kicked up their heels to the rhythm of the "saltarello..."(19)

Naturally, they came from the "Grotto of the Fairies," because they were...fairies!

These fairies also descended to Castelluccio, to Foce, to Rocca, to dance at night with the fresh masculine youth. And only at night, because if they were surprised in the village by the first light of day, there would be trouble for all of them. One time, caught by the incipient light of dawn dancing frenetically with the boys of Castelluccio, the fairies had to rush off at full speed up the mountain, like devastating furies. The band of gravel which cuts across Monte Vettore was caused by that ruinous flight of theirs and came to be called the "road of the fairies." (20)

They ran on the quick wing of the wind, grazing the rock with their goat's feet. Yes, that's right, goat's feet! The ethereal and agile handmaidens of the Sibyl, who moved in the dance like dragonflies, were truly bourne on goat's feet, well hidden under their long veils opening out bell shaped in the frenetic whirling of the dance.

And the people said:

> they are also beautiful, these fairies
> but their legs clatter like goats. (21)

No one could imagine that the pedestrian appendages of these beautiful women's bodies could consist of goat parts. When a mountaineer at Foce, surprised by the scratching of the feet of an enchanting fairy dancer, discovered in the place of the little glittering shoes of Cinderella, the two foul hooves of a goat, he was horrified and on the point of crying out against the diabolical fraud. But the infernal dancer whispered in his ear magical words:

"Don't speak! In exchange for your secrecy you will have immeasurable riches: every time you put your hand in your pocket, you will take it out laden with golden coins!"

And he did just that, for a long time. It's a shame that the mountaineer had to reveal the secret one day: in a second all the money he accumulated disappeared in a flash of lightening.(22)

The Intervention of the Authorities

Certain women of the Sibilline region, oscillating between the role of witch and that of astrologer/fortune teller, were not necessarily considered evil. As a matter of fact, they sometimes enjoyed the reputation of knowing how to foresee the future. There were various ones in Visso, especially in the 16th Century, as attested by Urbanite Cipriano Piccolpasso (1524-1579) in one of his reports.(23) They predicted the future, "by inclination of heaven" or by "spells," or by "witchery and other diabolical illusions." A certain Angeruta even foretold the pontification of Cardinal Farnese, who passed through these parts to go to the famous sanctuary of Mary of Macerato, and not in vain, because afterwards the Farnese indeed became Pope Paul III...

My goodness! They also wanted to gain the favor of the full ecclesiastical authority, and hopefully not to irritate them into a disagreeable frame of mind, which often ended up with some "bonfire" and the consequent smell of burning...

It is stupefying how widespread the practice of magical rites and foolish beliefs were in this particular Sibilline region, from Norcia to Visso, all the way to Montemonaco and beyond. The preachers thundered against the hardworking valley dwellers, threatening the wrath of God. Amongst them stands out St. Giacomo della Marca (+1476) merciless "hammer" of the Sibilline superstitions. He has left a flavorful test of conscience for poor souls, those lost to the urgings of shady sorcerers and bloodcurdling beliefs, calling them to plumb the most secret folds of the spirit according to this lively "outline:"

"If you believe in the fortune tellers and sorcerers. If you have believed that women or human bodies go about at night and become witches or cats or wolves and drink the blood of animals and like practices...if you have had books of spells and other similar things and if you do not burn them no one can give you absolution."

The religious authorities weren't joking. While falling short of the bonfires of one time, in an *Editto Generale del S. Offizio* of May 27, 1829, Dominican inquisitor D.A. Airenti threatened solemn excommunication of the meek inhabitants of Ancona in the Marches. That is, those who had not denounced, amongst others, the following individuals:

"Those who had done or were doing acts, by which one would infer an express or tacit pact with the devil, practicing spells, magic, sorcery or burning incense for finding treasures, and other ends; asking the devil questions and invoking him and to this effect promising him obedience, consecrating to him pentangles, books, swords, mirrors, or other things which partake of his name and work. Those who have meddled or are meddling in making experiments of necromancy and whatever other sort of magic with entrances into circles and making experiments with decanters and sieves to find some treasures, thus hidden, stolen, or lost, and do commit other similar superstitious actions and pursue such ends, with the maximum being the abuse of sacraments or of sacred or blessed things [...] Those who have books of necromancy, magic, or books containing spells, sorcery or similar superstitions, the maximum being the abuse of sacred things". (23/b)

Nobody escaped, as in a 1600's Spanish edict. The snarling *Editto,* in its interesting and particular examples, eloquently documents the ardent passion for necromancy and various magical rites of the sly people of Piceno.

Other Legends — Sinister or "Gilded"

Other legends have sinister, bloodcurdling flashes. One tells of the dark sentence against Pontius Pilate, condemned to live in craggy ravines where not even the echo of near and distant church bells could reach. Others speak of terrifying tempests around the accursed mountains. The terrified shepherds claimed to have seen, between the lightening flashes and the pelting water, the spirit of the wandering fairies like tongues of flame and the devil in person, wrapped in a black cloak with a plumed cap and two glowing eyes like embers. (24)

More innocuous are the legends of the treasures of the grotto, such as the one about a sow of gold with a brood of golden piglets, or a mother hen of gold with golden chicks, who chose, respectively, as a pigsty or as a chicken roost, nothing less than the inaccessible belly of the Sibilline grotto. Tomburi recalls with incomparable narrative mastery this "golden" legend.

The explorations in search of treasure did not always end happily. One time, for example, a bold adventurer descended into the belly of the grotto and was able to satisfy, for a second, his burning fever for gold. Faced with a glittering pile of inviting coin, he immediately filled his capacious pockets; but then the devil in person appeared implacably before him with those withering eyes. The unfortunate fellow, pale and trembling, emptied his pockets as fast as he could and fled precipitously:

> *Corre, zompa jo la valle,*
> *E 'gni zumpu le carcagne*
> *Je rtucchia le spalle*
> Run, jump down into the valley,
> And with every jump his heels
> Touch his back

But the devil croaked behind him:
"Put it down! Put it down!"
One coin remained entangled in the folds of his pockets and that was his ruin. He fell from a precipice and inhabitants of the village heard his tortured cries. They found him more dead than alive.

The treasure is still there in the stomach of the glittering grotto, and still waits for more gutsy men to go down there to seize it. They must, however, elude the guard of the ferocious devils.(25)

These are truly imaginative mountaineers, who also play loose with history, crediting the foundation of Montemonaco to no less than Charlemagne, or even back to the grandsons of Noah! (26)

Another charming legend, floral so to speak, related to Graf by professor Vincenzo Ghinassi, explains the origin of the Lago di Pilato. On the day the Jews crucified Jesus, the mountain people of the Sibillines noted that the grotto was abandoned by the Sibyl and that the lake had mysteriously turned blood red. Around the lake, as if by a miracle, the slope sprouted with leaves which resembled two joined hands. The mountaineers recognized in those leaves the hands of Jesus, joined together and pierced with a nail, a dark sign in their midst. But who had permitted those adored hands to be pierced through? Pilate, of course; so now that lake of bloody water was called Pilate's. (27)

Then there is the other legend which depicts a gentle, peaceful, industrious Sibyl, disposed to descend into the villages to teach the "maids" the art of spinning and other domestic skills, along with the more noble virtues. In her realm she herself is also very skillful at spinning and weaving, giving a good, and bewitching, example. (28)

These are remote legends which fade with the memories of the old mountaineers of today. Mixed together with others and tinged with new picturesque particulars, the stories undergo an incessant metamorphosis which wears them out and dissolves them for ever.

Many have already vanished with the death of the old common folk, who knew how to repeat them in the rhythmic singsong of a nursery rhyme.

Most young people don't know them anymore, because they consider them, justifiably, vaporous and fleeting myths, foolish and superstitious. They prefer other, more full-bodied myths, but they forget, perhaps, that inside the cocoon of the ancient legend is the diligent silkworm of eternal knowledge and the light butterfly of immortal poetry.

CHAPTER IV

ILLUSTRIOUS VISITORS
TO THE GROTTO AND TO THE LAKE

Since ancient times innumerable people have climbed up to the grotto, to the lake, or to both, as if visiting two sinister sanctuaries of the evil spirit. Mythical visitors and visitors who really existed are dealt with here. Almost all of them are shrouded in a dark cloud of mystery, driven by a restless passion for the unknown.

The first news of these disconcerting pilgrimages, limited to the lake, is from around the middle of the 14th century. But a tradition doesn't sprout from nothing. By the time it has entered the domain of literature, it must have already been part of the oral folklore, however feeble and imprecise. The official consecration and the spread of literary reputation comes from the authority of the writer, but the origin comes from the ardent imagination of the people. As soon as a writer captures a popular legend, a marriage is immediately performed between the native element and the literary reflection, to the full advantage of the legend itself.

As for the frequenters of the enchanted Sibilline region, it must be said that the first written memoirs refer to the lake. These speak generally of the visits of necromancers without specifying the name of any person in particular. Frightened climbers went up there in groups, because whether it was Pierre Bersuire or Fazio degli Uberti, they bore in mind that the defenses (including walls) and the vigilance surrounding the lake were aimed at obstructing their access.

On the other hand, the first written notice of the grotto's existence coincides with the arrival of a famous character in medieval chivalric literature: the *Guerin Meschino* of Andrea da Barberino, composed around 1410. (29) All of Chapter V is dedicated to the adventures of the hero in the Grotta della Sibilla, setting fire to a thousand fairytale lights.

Guerino's story is the slight and intriguing tale of a boy of princely origins, left orphaned at a tender age and passed from master to master. Always valorous and virtuous, but always grieving because he did not know who his parents were, he was considered a poor foundling, so much so as to receive the nickname of "Meschino" (wretched/poor). After fabulous victories in individual jousting and in battles, he decided to leave Constantinople, where he was in service to Alessandro, son of the emperor. Here he had felt his heart burn secretly for the princess Elissena. He wanted to leave because a knight, who he had defeated in battle, had spit these words in his face:
"You should be ashamed of yourself for not even knowing who your parents are!"

No one could detain Il Meschino, who took to the roads of the world to discover his parentage. But he wandered, wandered without end, until in Tunisia the solitary magician Calabach directed him to Alcina, the fairy who lived in the mountains of Italy.
He set sail for Calabria, where an old man informed him that Alcina lived in the mountains in the middle of Italy, near Norcia. He warned him that all the winds were up there, because that is where they are born, and that there were gigantic griffins.

After a confused voyage through the Mediterranean with landings in cities totally off the map, Guerino finally arrived in Norcia. He found lodgings with the innkeeper Anuello, who asked him;
"Where are you from?"
"I am going all over the world, and I don't know where I am from or

where I am going."

In this way the fable widens to a suggestive immensity.

At the inn they said that climbing to the cavern of the fairy was like choosing suicide. One fellow swore that he had seen three youths going up to the grotto: two of them returned, the third didn't. They also said that a certain Messer Lionello di Francia, for love of a damsel, ventured all the way to the cave of the grotto. He didn't go in, however, because a deadly wind flowed out which could have devoured the very stones of the mountain.

Thus according to the written tradition, the first visitors to the cave were shrouded in mystery simply because their story was shrouded in fable.

The innkeeper Anuello was fond of Il Meschino and decided to accompany him as far as the hermitage which lay only six miles from the grotto. With a horse, three loaves of bread, a little cheese and a flask of wine, they set off laboriously. After sixteen miles they reached the Castello, where the official, intractable and inflexible, barred their way. But the sad story of Il Meschino moved the heart of the "corporal" and the two continued on.

At the hermitage they knocked reverently, and a voice from inside responded:

"Jesus of Nazareth, help us!"

Three bent monks, with cross in hand, came to the door and cried:

"Turn back, accursed ones, deceived by vanity and ghosts! Why do you want to go and lose soul and body?"

The three hermits, however, fell silent at hearing the tearful tale of the knight. Still, they beseeched him not to venture into that mouth of hell, because only one who was in perfect possession of all the virtues would be able to resist the invincible spell of the fairy and her realm of illusions.

But Il Meschino had not left the court of Constantinople for nothing, and he brushed aside the words of the hermits, trusting in the pureness of his intentions. However, he submitted with humility and gratitude to one hermit's sermon instructing him in the virtues to practice in this realm of lust. To defeat the ardent seducers he must repeat in the most intoxicating and risky moments, "Jesus of Nazareth, help me!."

Il Meschino listened well, because the three hermits, grown old in this spot, had seen many enter the grotto and none come back out.

Provided with candles and flintstones, the hero started out for the prophetic cave alone, with a beating heart. But the way was steep, with fearful precipices. Scrabbling hand over hand along the ridge of sharp cutting rock, he did the best he could. His injured hands oozed drops of blood on the parched rock. He was at the point of turning back humiliated, when there came to his mind the short prayer taught to him by the hermit. Repeating it from his heart, he advanced towards the summit of the mountain, which appeared to be flung up high, up as far as the heavens. From the bottom, with the rocks grinding underfoot, the summit appeared so very far off, that one could barely make out a handkerchief of blue, up there, like a mirage.

He went on, making a great effort, breathing heavily, until a vast square space opened up in front of him, strewn with broken stones from above, like an immense cemetery of ruined tombs. Opposite there rose up a mountain higher than all the others, in which he could make out four obscure entrances, close by.

But by now the sun had set behind the peak and the shadows lengthened thickly in the desert of stone. He passed the night lying on the rocks. At the first light of dawn, he recited the seven penitential psalms with many other prayers. Then, with the candle lit, he went forward into one of the four caverns which further along reunited into one. Three times he found himself in front of enormous boulders that protruded from the mountain and cut the path, and three times he was forced to retrace his steps. The candles kept going out in his hand.

But with the help of the name of Jesus of Nazareth, he went forward!

After a stretch he heard ahead of him the thunder of raging water. Surprised, he stopped in his tracks. Guerino was very tired and chose to refresh himself with a little bread, along with some of the water from the

crashing stream. He ate and abandoned himself to a brief restorative nap. And
then onwards again, beyond the roaring but beneficial waters, with cautious
but decisive steps.

And then he felt under his feet a soft thing, like a sack of wool, and he
heard growl at him with the voice of a man:
"Who are you who tramples on me?"
Il Meschino leapt backwards and drawing his sword rebutted:
"Who are you who crosses my path?"
It was an enormous slimy snake, which writhed in the tunnel dark as
pitch. Hidden under the disgusting scales were the soul and body of Macco,
the wandering Jew, who told Guerino the horrendous misfortunes of his life.
He was a professional of vice, diabolically retaining the appearance of virtue.
At the age of thirty-three, disgusted with himself and with the others, he was
drawn to the adventure of the enchanted realm and knocked on the metal
door. But they didn't want to open it. He then swore: the final blasphemous
syllables had not slid from his foul mouth, when he had already begun to
uncoil in the loathsome form of a serpent.
"And remain here, cursed one!" the pure Meschino shouted at the undu-
lating back. From the pointed snout of the snake came a satanic hiss:
"You too could remain here! Like more than a hundred others who
remain confined here, of whom you in the world stupidly say that they are
enjoying themselves in the arms of the fairy!"

Il Meschino continued on to the metal door, guarded by two colossal figures of devils sculpted from bare rock. An inscription carved into the wall,
similar to that at the entrance of Dante's Inferno, froze Il Meschino:
"Who enters by this door and exceeds a year will not leave again,
  will not die until the day of Judgement; but then will perish in the
  body and will be damned in the soul."

The hermit had warned him of this; immediately Il Meschino repeated
the miraculous prayer. He then knocked on the polished metal door, which
opened to reveal the charms of three seductive damsels, their provocative

eyes murky with lust. Guerino divined in these fatal eyes temptation and derision, and put his spirit on guard, turning instinctively to his faithful sword.

When the door opened it was noon of June 16 of a year lost in the infinite silence of time. The girls gave him a festive reception; one took the flask of wine, the other the candle, the third replaced the sword in its sheath. Accompanying him to a world conjured up by phantasmagoric spells, they came to a veranda all decorated with historic scenes. Fifty young girls, lovelier than a dream, curtsied to him graciously, until a matron, the most beautiful woman that his pure eyes had ever contemplated, came to meet him with the attitude of love. A damsel announced in a voice of silver:

"Here is the great Madame Fairy!"

Guerino knelt before her, but she, with an agile and elegant bow, took him sweetly by the hand and whispered with gentleness:

"Welcome, messer Guerino!"

Guerino was hungry from the toil of his arduous journey; and behold, a table set with the most delicious foods appeared before his astonished gaze. But the hero recognized the temptation of gluttony and, invoking Jesus of Nazareth, dined on only bread and salt.

In one room of a majestic palace Alcina, splendid as a ray of sunshine, showed him her treasures: gold, jewelry, pearls, diamonds, which could make the head spin with their blinding brilliance. Then she took him into a garden overflowing with all the fruits imaginable, even those out of season. It was similar to Tasso's garden of Armida, which was also enchanted, where:

the breeze, like no other, is caused by the sorceress,
the breeze which makes the trees flower:
with eternal flowers the fruit lasts forever,
and while the one sprouts the other matures

(Gerusalemme Liberata, ch. XVI. st. 10).

But the hero, still spotless as a flake of snow, understood the duplicitous sorcery and braced his spirit with another prayer. He had descended into this enchanted realm, not for pleasure, but to learn news of his mother and father.

The queen, however, didn't give an answer, and stalled him with discussion and sorcery. She took him by the hand, while two girls called forth from a harp the most ecstatic harmonies and two others sang with the voices of sirens. The Fairy revealed her foul designs when, covering her face with the finest of veils, she fixed Il Meschino with eyes feverish with passion. And he, before a Medusa so dazzling, felt petrified and began to forget the stern warning of the hermit.

They entered a room shimmering with impossible beauty. The girls vanished like luminous shadows and the fairy tried to seduce him. Guerino saw that he was lost and when he invoked the name of Jesus of Narareth, a mysterious force pushed him out of the room. In vain the Fairy waited for him, until she was compelled to seek him out, to ask him why he had gone away from the very threshold of pleasure. Guerino, at this moment, understood that the Fairy could not know the secrets of the human heart.

Many other times Alcina attempted to subdue the pure Meschino with her infernal charms, but in vain, because the hero had an invincible weapon in that prayer to Jesus of Nazareth. One evening the enchantress, at the sound of that divine name, fled the room without knowing why. Aglow with love, she assailed with every possible means the unshakable virtue of the guest.

Guerino meanwhile implored her to reveal to him his parentage and she, diabolically, revealed to him that part of his life that he knew too well, to prove her magical powers. But when it came to the name of his father and mother, she immediately became mute, and Guerino despaired.

Alcina was explicit: he would know his real origin only by passing onto the path of sin. But Il Meschino did not sin. The Fairy had him dressed in silk and gave him a horse decked in splendor. She pointed out the richest realm, spangled with palaces, castles, gardens, and promised to make him lord of it. By then, however, he knew that everything was an infernal illusion.

Il Meschino was also tested by the temptation of sloth. Worn out with fatigue, he found himself in a bed soft as a caress, wrapped in a whirlwind of delirious perfume, while sweet smelling rose petals, moved by magical powers, brushed over his skin hardened on the fields of battle. To defeat the temptation Guerino had to punch himself. He stayed awake on his feet, hardly sleeping on the bare earth and remembering often the name of Jesus of Nazareth.

But the days passed and the Fairy did not reveal the secret of his parents. Softly she promised, and cruelly she withheld. She wanted to make him sin if only from impatience. However, the youth bore everything imperturbably, in the vain hope of an answer.

He began to get fed up with this realm. One Friday evening he was disgusted to see men and women change color, becoming pallid and fearful in their aspect. In the night he heard piercing laments and painful howling from these people, who had become invisible. The youth asked information about the strange phenomenon and a forty-six-year-old man explained to him that, by divine will, every Saturday the citizens of the enchanted realm were transformed into various beasts, according to the sins that they had been committing in this place of perdition. They kept these forms until Sunday dawn, when they returned to the splendor of before.

Guerino felt a shiver of horror, which grew when he saw the man change before his incredulous eyes into a ghastly dragon hissing horrible curses.

The earlier seductions resumed. In the seventh month the cave became a splendid court, of which Guerino was the king, revered by maidens and by poets who sang of his glorious exploits in battle. But he glimpsed in the sorcery the sin of pride, and he turned again to Jesus of Nazareth.

When the seventh month came to an end, he again asked Alcina to disclose to him the mystery of his birth, but she required in exchange that the youth invoke the gods of Egypt and Chaldea. Then Il Meschino, seeing that every attempt was in vain, and afraid of the intensification of the seductions, prepared to leave. In one day the queen renewed all the temptations together, in a desperate round of madness, and he was only saved by invoking the name of Jesus.

"You will regret it," cried the Fairy, infuriated, "but if you want to, you can leave!"

"I want to!" replied Il Meschino.

And immediately a terrifying earthquake shook the cave. In an abyss the hero saw all the most disgusting and filthy beasts: they were the souls of those whom the Fairy had subjugated with her fatal spell.

The last day a damsel led him to the door through which he had entered, because by the will of Heaven she was obliged to indicate the hour and the place of exit from the realm of deception. Nevertheless the damsel with persuasive and tender ways still sought to detain the hero, promising him the pardon of the Fairy.

Guerino's answer was to leap through the door. He heard called at his back:

"Go, and may you never find your parentage!"

And he in response: "Go and tell the Fairy that I am alive and will live, I am cheerful and I will save my soul!"

She shut the door and Il Meschino commended her to the Lord.

When he met Macco again, they exchanged scornful words. He recrossed the roaring river, leaped outside of the cave, and laughed under the sky laden with stars.

He arrived at the hermitage and knocked. The hermits and Anuelo believed it was a trick of the devil, but for charity's sake they opened the door and saw Il Meschino. They cried out at the miracle and sang hosannas to the virtue of the hero.

Guerino took the road to Rome to present himself to the Pope, who asked him with what intentions he had dared to enter the castle of Alcina. When he knew the truth, the Pontif pardoned him, gave him 200 pieces of gold, and for penitence, ordered him to go to the sanctuary of St. Giacomo di Compostella, with the task of defending from marauders the helpless pilgrims on their way there.

And here falls the curtain on the legend of Guerin Meschino, as far as it relates to the Grotta della Sibilla. We chose to retell it in its particulars—but also freely—since it deals with a legend dear to our people. It was very well known at one time, because odd buskers repeated it in coarse verses during the fairs and festivals of our villages. And it passed from mouth to mouth in the festive carousel of ballads during the idle evenings of winter, around the hearth.

Thus it deals with a legend that is the foundation of the enchanting splendors of the grotto, the first and the richest of the magical elements. And away with you, without the shadow of a doubt, just like a fairy tale.

The Sire of Pacs and the Great-Uncle of Gaulchier de Ruppes

We aren't going to repeat the history of the German knight and his page, who plunged back into the sensual arms of the Queen Sibilla to feed on drunken pleasure until the end of the world, let it cost what it may, even their souls; nor the history of the five youths of Montemonaco, saved by their unconquerable fear before the blast of wind; nor that of the priest, Antonio Fumato, who wisely didn't want to advance his foot one centimeter towards the metal doors, abandoning the two Germans to their fate. We pause instead to narrate briefly the history of the Sire of Pacs or Paques, as related by De La Sale.

That noble French Sire had a young brother who longed for knightly adventures, was passionate about travel, and was always in search of mysterious and enchanted places. The youth, during one of his many voyages, arrived at the splendid city of Ancona, and asked if it was true, as they said, that the Grotta della Sibilla was in the Anconese Marches. After he was told yes, there was no use trying to deter him from his plan of exploring the grotto. His traveling companions, having advised him against it, took advantage of a passing boat from Ancona headed for Rhodes, and sailed towards the East. But he, alone and intrepid, wanted to cross into the realm of the Sibyl. Thus he disappeared without a trace into the fatal sanctuary of the Fairy Queen.

Around 1380 the news of his disappearance into the grotto reached the Sire di Pacs, who with anguish in his heart prepared a voyage to track down his beloved brother. Before undertaking the difficult climb of the witch's mountain, he wanted the benediction of the Pope and a safe conduct pass from the Captain of Montemonaco, so as to guarantee, morally and legally, the purity of his intentions.

A local man, Cola dell'Amandola, served as a guide; later he was personally interrogated by Antoine De La Sale. The Sire entered into the cave with the apprehension of spirit of one who loves unto death. When he traced his brother's name inscribed on the rock, his torment was indescribable. He began to scratch furiously at that inscription in order to obliterate the shame on his house. With an unconsolable cry, he lamented all at once the sudden disgrace of his noble family by the horrible undertaking of the reckless brother, the loss of a dear relative, and the misfortune of his parents for having given life to a son so degenerate.

So great was the pain that he fell unconscious into a soporific swoon. And he dreamt. In his dream he saw his brother again, alive, seated at the table with his two sisters. He took the dream for reality and departed with his heart overflowing with joy, towards the country where the people speak "oc" (Langue d'Oc), after thanking his courteous companions and giving his sword to the Captain of Montemonaco.

According to De La Sale, a great-uncle of Gaulchier de Ruppes had also entered the Grotta della Sibilla. Antoine wrote that in 1422, finding himself in Rome, he met with various illustrious persons, among them Gaulchier, all of whom were curious to hear about his excursion to the Grotta della Sibilla. Signor Gaulchier especially wanted to know about it, because, he said, one of his great-uncles had entered the grotto. On returning to his homeland, this great-uncle was grief-stricken by bad news, so much so that he decided to plunge back into the realm of the Sibyl and lose himself forever in the pleasures and riches, which he had habitually exaggerated in his astonishing conversations.

Antoine De La Sale also mentions that in the first square space of the grotto, where a few rays of light still penetrated, the names of various people, originating from many regions of Europe, were engraved in the rock. The inscriptions were already in great part eroded and obscured by the dampness of the rocks. Two, nevertheless, could be deciphered: that of a certain Her Hans Wan Banborg "intravit," who had penetrated into the grotto (but did he come out of it?) and that of a certain Thomin de Pons or de Pous, of whom it isn't known if he entered or exited the cave.

Antoine too, when he climbed up there the 18th of May 1420, wanted to leave inscribed "his motto and his maxim" on the hard rock of the grotto. A careful man, we must repeat that he did not go beyond the square space and that he was provided with a permit for the expedition granted to him by the qualified authority in Montemonaco. He did not want his name as a knight sullied by gossip describing him as reckless or wizard-like, because he, beyond everyone else, did not believe in these fairytales.

Simplicianus and Daniele

Some years before Antoine, between 1410 and 1413 approximately, a Swiss person with the obscure name of Simplicianus might have climbed to the grotto, in an adventure very similar to that of the German as told by De La Sale. Felix Hemmerlin gave a report of it, related in horrible Latin better adapted to describing the roughness of the Sibilline rocks than to evoking the fascinating legends of the grotto. (30)

His fairytale drips with lust. Not for nothing he calls the Monte della Sibilla, Mountain of Venus (Venusberg). And why? Because according to Hemmerlin it is said that Venus, wife of Vulcan, perpetually exercised her "venereum officium non sine calore" (function of Venus, not without heat/passion) there, and because "incubi e succubi," malign spirits who assume the appearance of women of an invincible beauty, live there, laying traps of feverish sensuality for men whom they draw from everywhere.

Hemmerlin describes with satisfaction the horrid landscape of the Monte della Sibilla, which according to him rises between Norcia and Montefortino. When a living person crosses the gorges of the mountain an infernal storm of thunder and hail is unleashed, grim enough for the places thereabouts. Caverns and caves riddle the rocks with meandering subterranean trenches.

While Hemmerlin was in Bologna the anti-pope John XXIII was staying there with his court. He knew that the friend of a certain knight wanted to meet the Pontif to plead for the pardon of a very serious sin committed by his friend. Which sin? The friend had lived an entire year in the grotto of the Sibyl, immersed up to his eyes in lascivious pleasures, imbibing "apud succubus e famellas Veneris".

The same friend then, namely Simplicianus, confessed to entering with two other companions, all of them bewitched by the enchanted atmosphere. Inside of a translucent and most agreeable space, resembling an immense quadrangular cathedral, were twelve distinct doors in the apses, fantastically ornamented. These doors were always ajar, all twelve months of the year, to the lusts of men.

They climbed the mountain in the month of March, and in the month of September, decked in gaudy foliage, they entered into the cave of the Sibyl. They sated themselves with heavenly delicacies while wrapped in an atmosphere saturated with perfume and intoxicating pleasure. Of the three, only Simplicianus succeeded in escaping, thanks to the apparition of an old man who explained to him various secrets of that world of sorcery, including the law according to which whoever stays more than a year in the grotto can never leave.

He told of having seen a host of innumerable persons, from every region, (especially from England), condemned to stay there eternally. He had seen, amongst the others, an aged gentleman with his son, agitated and alone, no longer participating in the crazy lusts of the others, because they were already thinking too much of their supreme destiny.

Simplicianus, contrite of heart for his sins, obtained the pardon of the Pope, unlike the German knight of Antoine De La Sale. And he prayed to God and the Virgin for his two companions hopelessly ensnared in the fatal seductions of the dreamy realm of the Sibyl.

Similar to the story of the German knight told by A. De La Sale, and more so to that of Tannhäuser with which it should be identified, is the tragic adventure of a certain Daniele, told by A. Oertel (1527-1598) in his *Theatrum Orbis Terrarum* (1572). (31)

The writer called the Monte della Sibilla "The Mountain of Venus" (Frau Venus Berg). He records that various popular German songs tell the story of the young man, Daniele, who after living in the cave of the Sibyl, went to ask pardon from the Pope. The Pope thrust his staff of dry wood into the ground and answered that Daniele would receive absolution only if the staff flowered. Despairing, Daniele vanished into the grotto, taking with him two nephews. After three days the staff flowered, but no one knew anything about the desperate youth. Oertel concluded: "it is thought that he spent the rest of his life in the grotto."

L. Pulci and G. delle Piatte

At the end of 1470 and beginning of 1471, the poet Luigi Pulci went to the enchanted places of the Sibillines with a much better psychological attitude. Subtle of spirit and rather skeptical, he was nevertheless sensitive to the fascinating call of the occult arts. He speaks of it in a letter to Lorenzo di Medici (32) dated Dec. 4, 1470, and in some verses in his *Morgante* (c.XXIV, stanze 112-13).

But for Pulci, one deduces from his verse, it was all a "beautiful game" in sympathetic memory of Cecco d'Ascoli. Perhaps Cecco climbed up there between the last decades of the 1200's and the first of the 1300's, when the legends of the Sibillines were still wrapped up in obscurity. Eventually tradition called him an annual visitor to the Lago di Pilato with his "book of commands," and author of one of the circles traced on a rock at the lake.

With the story of Giovanni delle Piatte of Trentino we plunge again from the subtle curiosity of the Florentine Pulci into the heaviest medieval witchcraft. Bonomo mentions Giovanni in one of his interesting essays on the

Caccia alle Streghe (Witch Hunt) drawing from a trial instituted against that bizarre sorcerer of Trentino in 1504 (but the events referred to occurred in about 1487). (33)

No less a magician than a friar, Giovanni one day decided with his master in cowl to climb, in impious pilgrimage, to the Monte della Sibilla or of Venus, call it what you will, where "the Lady Herodiades lives (sic dicta)."

They walked and walked; after three days the two finally arrived at the foot of a little blue pool, which had limpid reflections like the lakes of Trentino. But here on the bank appeared "a big friar, dressed in black, and he was black," who explained to them the essential condition for passing to the other shore of the lake: repudiate God, the Virgin, and their Christian faith..
Giovanni did not think twice and repudiated everything. Onwards along the risky paths of sorcery, they crossed through the doors that perpetually slammed, and over a slimy serpent who put himself in the way of their frenzied journey.

But at the entrance of another door Giovanni and the friar encountered an old man, "el fido Ekart," who informed the visitors of the laws which were in force in the realm: no one could ever leave again, once a full year had expired from the date of entry. They knew that!
Delle Piatte recounted at the trial that he had seen there an old man with a white beard, who slept a mysterious sleep, with his head resting on a table: it was Tannhäuser. There lived women and youths and men and there reigned the "Lady Venus" of the name Herodiades, prodigal dispenser of every delight of the senses.

But the master friar explained to his disciple: every week on Saturday, Sunday and up until noon on Monday, Venus was transformed into a serpent from the waist up; afterwards she returned a woman "et mena molte belle donzelle."
And who could hold Giovanni back? On Thursday night of the "Quattro tempora"(Ember Days) of Christmas, he plunged headlong for the first time

into those muddy waters of sensual pleasure. Eight more times he entered the warm alcove of Venus, making with her and her company a tour of the world: "on a black horse by air, and in five hours we circled the whole world." And they always stopped at crossroads and triple-cross-roads to eat, to drink exquisite wines, and to dance orgiastically. The witches of Val Sugana also participated in the cavalcade. These witches lived in service to the devil, a good employer who would "give three *quatrini* for one as wages".

The adventure of the wizard of Trentino synthesized admirably the scattered elements of the legend of the grotto, from Andrea da Barberino and Antoine De La Sale onwards. It also added the suggestive particulars of the nocturnal ride across the heavens, around the earth, and of the sinister outings of Venus to the crossroads, particulars already noted in the tradition of witchcraft.

Arnolfo di Harff and the New Times

In a confused and imprecise story, especially regarding the places near the Monte della Sibilla, Arnolfo di Harff tells of his attempt in the spring of 1497 to climb to the enchanted grotto. But he did not succeed. After reconnoitering pointless turns amongst caverns, grottos, heaps of stones, and puddles, and after being laughed out of Castellano where they made fun of his fancies, he and his traveling companions were forced to leave those inaccessible rocks.

But who can say that the story of Arnolfo was not a likable boast, as Reumont and Desonay supposed, the gallant inventions of a knight who did not want to be less than Tannhäuser or Il Meschino? (34)

In the 15th century there was a continual stream of visitors, as many to the grotto as to the lake. Regarding this, Alberti tells how the "Norsini" (of Norcia) were constrained "to close the aforesaid cavern and then to keep watch at the lake".

He also wrote that "some men from distant countries came to these places to consecrate wicked and foul books to the devil in order to fulfill some of their contemptible desires, such as riches, honors, delightful pleasures and similar things".

Those foolish visitors, properly hoodwinked by popular rumor, told tall tales so as not to be made fun of, informing everyone they had "obtained that which they were seeking".

Alberti, along with Razzano (1420-1492), lets us know that "some Germans, learned and experienced men", climbed up to the lake with proud necromantic intentions. But notwithstanding that for three whole days they repeated diabolical rites at the top of their voices, the demons, perhaps frozen in the icy waves of the lake, remained silent in the mysterious watery depths. In the end, those "scholarly" and stupid Germans departed for their remote lands, cursing their own slow-witted credulity and those who had spread such idiotic necromantic fables. (35)

At this point, the dawning of the 1500's, the fertile season of the Sibilline fables began to fade. There had already been an inkling of this in Pulci and even more so in the episode of Arnolfo di Harff. By now both the poet and the lord of the castle smile with the air of the new man who has gaily freed himself from coarse medieval tales.

But would you want the noble minds of the Renaissance to believe in legends of enchanted grottos? They wrote of them with enthusiastic rapture, with rare poetic intensity, as in Ariosto and in Tasso. But this was not because they believed in them. They wanted to smile over them, or to take from them the spark to ignite the kindling of their poetic evocations. They wanted to find in them the pretext for joyous escape into fairytale times, lost forever with the arrival of the gnawing woodworm of rationalism, or they wanted to voluptuously enjoy those residual portions of the unknown which always influence the human spirit.

The new minds no longer believed, as opposed to the common people who were still superstitious and dreaming. Thus in the second half of the 1500's, the 1600's, and the 1700's, the visits to the grotto and the lake were

increasingly rare. (36) After the 1500's, except for a few flickers, the literature was sadly silent about the grotto, which crumbled and filled up with
heaps of rocks, and about the lake, which languished in the solitude of its
frigid heights.

The rare visits were motivated now only by scientific interests. In 1557
Ulisse Aldrovandi, a highly regarded botanist from Bologna, undertook an
exploration of our mountains with the aim of learning the unexpected character-
istics of the rich flora, already noted with admiration by Antoine De La Sale.
The same was done for the same reasons by the Roman botanist Luigi Squalerno
Anguillara in 1506, the German naturalist Giambattista Winther in 1624, the
Florentine Pierantonio Micheli in 1708, Paolo Spadoni in 1807, etc. (37)
They were all scholars intent on discovering the secrets of the health-giving
herbs of these mountains. It was as if the mountains wanted to introduce into
natural science a pinch of mystery and also of miraculousness, as if to take
revenge on science itself for having been denuded of the enchanted fairytales
of one time.
And sometimes these mountains entrusted the vendetta to the neighbors
of Castelluccio, who, for example, in 1892 mistook an innocuous botanist for
a wizard, and came close to lynching him.

The bloody fairytale, then, is followed by bloodless science. However, at
the end of the 19th century, when noted scholars made pilgrimages to the
grotto and the lake to verify the early tales of Andrea da Barberino, Antoine
De La Sale, Felix Hemmerlin etc., a new literary season of the Sibilline legends began. But it is philology in the place of poetry, which lives secretly in
the pages of ancient writers, or still slithers in a dying hiss from the lips of
some old mountaineer.

CHAPTER V

THE SIBILLINE LEGENDS IN LITERATURE

Having come this far, we want to make a short "excursus" into the literary history of the myths of the grotto and the lake. This should give a glimpse of the unsuspected interest in the subject matter on the part of various poets and writers, including famous ones. We will touch on only the most noted, in order not to "lower the prestige" of the roll. To avoid the boring repetition of erudite nursery rhymes, we won't mention the authors already studied in the preceding chapters, like Pierre Bersuire, Andrea da Barberino, Antoine De La Sale, Felix Hemmerlin, etc.

The First Poets Of the Lake: Fazio degli Uberti and Luigi Pulci

Among the poets, the first to respond to the roll call is Fazio Degli Uberti with his *Dittamondo*, composed in stages between 1346 and 1367.

Fazio imagined a fantastic journey around the three parts of the world, undertaken as an incitement to Virtue and in the company of the ancient geographer Solino. He describes countries and districts, recollects histories and personalities, in a sequence of frozen moralizing allegories. His verse is descriptive and flowing, but without an inner lyrical movement.

Fazio, the good Tuscan, takes pleasure in teasing the "marchisani" like Boccaccio and Sachetti (because the Tuscans have always looked down their noses a little at the Marchigiani; even Michelangelo, who was embittered against Raphael and more so against his fellow countryman "patron" Bramante). He actually made the Marches nothing less than the homeland of Judas:

> "Enter the Marches, as I recount,
> I saw Scariotto, from whence was Judas
> According to the saying of some, of which was recounted." (38)

The scholars tried to find some villages in the Marches that sound like "Scariotto", and Crocioni thought of Montecarotto, which in the Latin genitive sounds as "Montiscarotti". (39)

In some verses ascribable to around 1360, Fazio, more attentive to strange fables than to the true beauties of the Piceno region, also recalls the necromantic repute of the Lago di Pilato:

> The reputation here will not remain unadorned.
> Of the Mount of Pilate, where there is a lake
> Which watches the summer moult its feathers,
> Therefore Simon Mago, intending
> To sanctify his book, climbed up there,
> Where there was a tempest with great turbulence,
> According to what was recounted of up there.
> (Book III, chapter 1) (40)

These pale and colorless verses have more importance as documents than as poetry, because when it came to poetry, Fazio didn't understand much.

Another Tuscan poet, the above cited Pulci, could sing of the lake's necromantic riches because he had visited it personally. His feeling about the occult here oscillates between the "beautiful game" and passionate curiosity, many times sinfully satisfied. In his *Morgante Maggiore* discoursing in general on lawfulness and on the power of magic and spells, at a certain point he exclaims:

> Thus I want to disclose little by little
> That I was at the Mountain of the Sibyl,
> Which to me seemed for a while a beautiful game;
> There still remains in my heart some sparks
> Of seeing again the many enchanted waters,
> Where already the Ascolano Cecco pleased me.

And Moco and Scabro and Marmores then
and the bifurcated bone which opened up
searching, like one does when one's in love;
this was my Parnassus and my muses;
and say of it I am guilty and know that
If there is another assembly like at Grand Minos I will forgive myself
and recognize the truth with the other wanderers,
pyromancers, hydromancers and geomancers.
(Chapter XXIV - verses 112-13) (41)

It is clear that Pulci "seeks" the secrets of magic by studying *Acerba* by
Cecco d'Ascoli (IV,4), because Moco, Scabro, and Mamores are the mysterious names of diviners, recorded so precisely by the Ascolane poet, together with "l'osso bifurcato," the pectoral bone of the rooster.

Pulci must have had quite a passion for magic if he sought it "like one
does when one is in love." The necromantic language confirms this, especially in that last verse stretched at a gallop like a fiery colt:

"Pyromancers, hydromancers, and geomancers."

All of these are devilish people, claiming to foresee the impossible
future in the flicker of flames and the tails of burning meteors, or in the
strange actions of water, or through cabalistic signs drawn on the ground.

The Gifted Caracciolo

At the close of the 15th century a gifted poet of the Neapolitan court,
Pierantonio Caracciolo, wrote peculiar verses about the necromancers of the
Sibillines in his *Farsa dello Ymagico*. (42) This farce was performed in the
presence of his Majesty Don Ferrante I of Aragon with "Pyrrantonio in the
role of a magician: he went on stage first in a toga with his face and beard in
the ancient style of high authority, accompanied by four disciples dressed in
white. The first carried a branch of gold, as a symbol of that which the Sibyl

Enea had, the second a book of magical arts. Another carried a big vase that contained fire and incense, the fourth had an unsheathed knife, a magical instrument with which to make circles".

There you are: the magical and witchy atmosphere is created with the tools and ingredients of the trade. The necromancer wants to present himself with his papers in order as a skilled and honest laborer, informing the spectators with the coarse boisterous verses.

Of this I speak like some who say
that often they go to Norcia
to find,
caverns and grottos
well guarded
by enchanted serpents
and by centaurs;
then they speak of big treasures
they have found
and consecrated books;
and also at the end
mountains of rubies
and of diamonds,
guarded by giants,
and in the midst of them
a bed all of gold,
where there is sun
resting with the sun
Diana;
and the fairy Morgana
then shows herself
and everybody embraces
and caresses
and they are given meat,
and from that milk
everyone returns remade

those people.
And so well contented
they go from there
at the end of the year
to their own homes.

Here the literary elements of the Sibilline legend mix themselves with accents of a tasty popular flavor, for that flux and reflux of motifs which initially arise from the lips of the people, then flow together in the writers' work and from there flow back again filtered through the creative lips of the enchanted realm.

The Humanist Scholars

But do not think that in the 15th century only lovers of magic, or bizarre poets, were interested in the Sibilline legends. Some humanist scholars, disdaining the common language and expressing themselves in high flown pompous Latin, used them in their own way.

The series begins with Enea Silvio Piccolomini, who later became Pope under the name Pio II. He remembered the grotto in a letter to his brother Giorgio in 1431 in an exquisite Latin. The Monte della Sibilla is described as not far from the City of Norcia:

"Ubi praeruptus mons ingentum speluncam facit, per quam aquae fluunt. Illic memini audisse me striges esse et demones ac nocturnas umbras, ubi, qui audaces animo sunt, spiritus vident alloquunturque et artes edicunt magicas; haec non vidi nec videsse curavi, nam quod peccato discitur, melius est ignorasse." (43)

"Where the mountain, torn away, makes a huge cave, through which waters flow. There I remember having heard there to be owls and demons and nocturnal ghosts, where those who are daring in character see and talk to spirits and learn thoroughly magic arts; these things I neither saw nor troubled myself to have seen, for what is learned through sin it is better to be ignorant of".

In the discreet hands of the shrewd humanist, the dark medieval fable fits into a framework of classical decorum, notwithstanding the traditional demoniacal elements and the surprising credulity of the author.

In his quick and sober description of the mountain landscape (rent though it is by a huge cave with water running through it), he doesn't appear to be affected by the dreadful harshness of the route, as Hemmerlin, for example, was. The characters who populate the grotto and the daring ones who break into it, including witches, demons, and necromancers, who see and speak with the spirits and learn the magical arts, seem to live in distant and serene memories. His only worry is this final moralizing touch: that which one learns by sin, is better to have never known.

Around the years 1448-1453 another cultured humanist was pleased to fleetingly record the legends of the Sibillines. Flavio Biondo, in his work, *Italia Illustratae*, speaks of high mountains, remote and inaccessible, into which the cavern of the Sibyl opens. A little further up lies the Lago di Pilato, which brims with fish that are demons, as in the fairytales. It is the arduous destination of necromancers eager to grasp the unknown:

> *"Altissimis vero in montibus qui praedictis oppidis e regione respondent summo in Appennino est mons Santae Mariae in Gallo {=Montegallo}, oppidum cui ipso in Appennino propinqua est caverna, Sybillae vulgo appelata; et paulo superius est lacus ille, in Nursinorum agri Apennino, quem vano ferunt mendacio piscium loco daemonibus scatere. Ea tamen duorum locorum fama multos et plures superioribus, ut audivimus, saeculis pellexit necromantia delectatos aut noscendarum rerum mirandarum avidos ut arduos hos montes magno vanoque labore conscenderent."* (44)

> "In the high hills of the Appenine uplands, directly opposite these towns just mentioned, lies the town of Monte Santa Maria in

Gallo {=Montegallo}. Near this town, in the Appenines themselves, is a huge cavern commonly called the Cave of the Sibyl,
and a little higher up, that lake in the Norcian Appenines which
is quite falsely said to teem with demons instead of fish. Yet the
repute of the two places has driven many in our day (and many
more in earlier centuries, as I heard) to climb these daunting hills
with great effort, but all in vain, captivated by sorcery or eager to
acquaint themselves with marvels."
(Translated by Jeffrey A. White)

In his elaborate Latin dictation Biondo offers precious news about the
prehistory of these legends, which, with respect to when he was writing
(about 1450) would have already been some centuries old: "Superioribus sae-
culis" (From the greater era). (45)

Battista Spagnoli, called the Mantovano (1444-1516), recalls the
bewitched Sibilline Mountains in "well constructed" Latin hexameters. (He
is noted too for some of his writings about the transfer of the Holy House
of Loreto). He speaks of it in certain hexameters of 1513, dedicated to St.
Nicola da Tolentino. While discussing the devils that assail in all ways the
heroic virtue of St. Nicola, he observes in passing that they gathered like a
convention under the ancient peak, where it was rumored that the Sibyl
lived within gloomy caverns. As he expressed this in Latin:

Isti omnes igitur coetu in sublime vocato,
Culmen in obscuris vetus est ubi fama Sybillam degere speluncis...

In the same composition he writes that the Sibyl had sojourned "sub
specubus piceis," that is, in caves black as pitch. (46)

It is the commemoration of an erudite humanist and moralistic poet,
overly literary, without the earlier inspiration of the beautiful fairytale.

Similarly, one reads the polished Latin couplets in the *Picenum* by
Panfilo of San Severino Marche, who died in 1542. He begins with descrip-

tions of the suggestive landscape of the Sibillines, concluding with a reference to the necromantic rites at the lake:

Montibus at contra Gallus respondit in altis
Non procul ex antro, Diva Sibylla, tuo.
Poma dabit cerasi praecocia maius apricis,
Hic tibi sextilis vix ea dona feret.
Hic antiqua manet lapidoso vertice quercus,
Quae retinet frondes tempus in omne suas,
Nubibus assiduis st vertice sidera pulsat.
Quod superat cunctos, nomina Victor habet.
Hic lacus ille suas extendit frigidus undas,
Quem necromantes nocte dieque petunt.
Dicitur in cyclo Tau, Erux, variusquee character
Quae referant Summi nomina sacra Jovis. (47)

Translated these solemn verses sound something like this:

Opposite, on the high mountains, is Monte Gallo,
Not far from your cavern, oh divine Sibyl.
May, in sunny places, will bring the
early fruits of the cherries, and only the
sixth month, up there, will bring a gift to you.
Here, in the rocky heights, the aged oak
which keeps its leaves in every season, endures.
And with its top in persistent clouds, touches the stars.
The mountain taller than all the others is called Vettore.
Here is that famous lake which spreads its frozen waves,
And is visited night and day by necromancers.
In the middle of a circle one pronounces Tau, Erux,
and an intricate fire iron marks the sacred names of the highest Jove.

From the documentary point of view, the Latin prose passages of Nicolo

Peranzoni, in his *De Laudibus Piceni* composed between 1510 and 1527, can be regarded as more important. (48)

The author illustrates the traditions of the grotto and the lake with the critical spirit of the humanist disposed to smile at the "foolish and credulous common people." The common people, he writes, think that the Cumaen Sibyl lives in the grotto. The same one who accompanied Aeneas at Averno and who instructed the Madonna in the sacred letters, is now condemned to remain in this cavern until the Day of Judgement.

Many, desiring to know the future, enter the grotto, but leave disappointed. Worse, they return in a sorry state because the shepherds in these mountains fall upon them and "fleece" them by force.

Peranzoni discusses the ancient Sibyl and the mountainous place where at one time she exercised her office of prophetess, observing that by now all is lost in the mists of time. If in certain mountains one can find inexplicable phenomena, they must be considered "fantastical and diabolical illusions." And one can't exclude that the inaccessible caverns could be hideouts for alchemists, who, observed by no one, could coin false money there.

As for the Lago di Pilato, Peranzoni, after recording that a crowd of necromancers went up there to consecrate "the book of commands," observes that there are two reasons for its infernal fame. First of all, its geographical position renders it totally isolated from the rest of the world and therefore particularly suitable for the dangerous necromantic rites. Secondly, there are the two magical circles inscribed in the rock close to the waters of the lake, traced, according to the gossip, one by Virgil and the other by Cecco d'Ascoli.

According to the foolish popular tale, the lake had acquired the name of Pilate when the body of the Roman proconsul, dragged by two bulls, sank into the rocky ground and the bloody mirror of water miraculously rose. Thus the mountaineers also call the lake "Bitaurum," because two bulls (bini tauri) sank into the ground with the body of the unfortunate Pilate, leaving some grooves in the rock, marks of the prophetic cart still visible at that time.

The learned Nicolo turned up his nose at the silly fairytale of the mountaineers and enlisted his philological weapons to demonstrate that in this case

"Pilato" is derived form the Latin "pilaris": "pro pilari lacus dictus est Pilatus" (the lake was called Pilatus after a vase). He argues: we know that "pila" signifies not only a concave vase but also any orb-shaped object. Since this lake is orb-shaped and situated on a high peak, in the beginning it was called "lacus Pilaris" and following the alteration of pronunciation (a frequent phenomena amongst ignorant people) it became "lacus Pilati," that is Lago di Pilato.

From the flights of the necromantic fairytale one passes to the flights of philology.

Some pages of the already cited Leandro Alberti (written before 1535) concern themselves with this document, whether for the legends, or for the description of the dramatic Sibilline landscapes and the phenomena of the waters of the lake "which rise and fall (...) in such a manner that everyone marvels who sees it, seeming to them something supernatural, not understanding the cause of such movement." (49)

Other authors, like Magini and Merula, underlined this singular phenomenon. We moderns would be curious to know what science has to say today about the oscillations of the waters of the Lago di Pilato. (50)

All these writers, perhaps, have an understandable moral preoccupation with wanting to refute the diabolical and deceptive legends. But they don't always succeed in containing their secret fascination, and sometimes end up by prattling in the presence of the glowing fable of infernal flashes and magical hallucinations. One verse of Lodovico "della tranquillita" is enough to overshadow all of them.

A Verse of Ariosto and Many of Trissino

I say one verse only, because in his work *Orlando Furioso* Lodovico Ariosto recorded fleetingly, but for eternity, the Grotta della Sibilla. He wrote that many able painters of the ancient and modern eras have admirably portrayed the things that have already happened, but no one has succeeded in depicting future events. Only one who has been ordained by the devil with the book of magic can depict things to come. Merlin did so by means of the work of the demons, thanks to his magic book, consecrated at the Lake Avernus and in the Sibilline "grottos":

> But you never hear of the ancients
> having painted the future–nor
> is this evident in any contemporary work.
> And yet scenes have been discovered
> that were depicted before they actually took place.
>
> But let no painter of old or of today
> boast that he can do this:
> even art must yield here to simple magic
> which causes tremors to the spirits in hell.
> Now this hall I mentioned in the last canto was painted
> in a single night by demons summoned by Merlin
> with his book–consecrated at Lake Avernus or else
> in the cave in Norcia.

(Canto XXXIII, stanze III-IV) (51)

Only one verse! But it is the most authoritative signature on the Sibilline legend from the most imaginative bard of witchcraft and magic.

Giangiorgio Trissino also took on this subject, with many more verses, indeed almost a whole book, but with much less authority and with little poetic inspiration. Trissino attributed to Ariosto's epic ballad the artistic failure of his own poem, *L'Italia Liberata dai Goti*, exclaiming angrily:

> Cursed be the day and the hour when
> you take the pen and don't sing of Orlando.

But the native defect was in the pen; how could his have constructed the swordplay adventures of Orlando?

Giangiorgio was nonetheless an honest and cultured scholar of the first half of the 1500's. Therefore, in his *L'Italia Liberata dai Goti* (1547-1548), he does not forget the myths of the Sibillines to which he dedicated all of Book XXIV:

In twenty-four he took himself to the Sibyl, he announces in the summary. And in fact, therein he relates that the "clever" Narsete, who arrived at Norcia to suppress the civil strife of the city, expressed the desire to go up to the cavern of the Sibyl:

> Burning with an incredible desire
> To visit our dear Sibyl
> Ancient in years and prudence;
> Of which by the grace of heaven conceded to her,
> She can know all the human things
> Which are, which were, and which must come.
> Up there is
> ... the cavern high and deep
> Of our ancient Sibyl
> To whom a number of people were in the habit of going.

But few were able to return from the "deep cavern," and among the few was S. Benedetto, who in this regard has left useful suggestions to the adventurous.

A bit more suggestive is the description of the Lago di Pilato with its nymphs and with its enchanted "palaces," with its dangerous labyrinths which swallow the visitors, and its waters populated by fish-demons:

> In this our frigid country
> One finds a mountain which has the name Vittore,
> Because it surpasses in altitude every other mountain;
> On that side which is towards the east

74

One finds a lake whose livid waters
Are full of demons that look like fish,
Which are always darting between those shores.

From those spacious caverns, fatal funnels which swallow men like grapes, one can escape through a secret hole which flows straight to Amatrice, at the border with the Ascolano territory:

By a hole near to Amatrice. (52)

Touched by the pen of Trissino, dripping with doctrine, even the most elegant fable freezes and expires.

The Bizarre Florentine Spirits: Berni, Aretino, Cellini, and Doni

However, the fable is revived and colored with a glittering fascination by the lightening sketches of some "bizarre Florentine spirits".

Berni recollects it and laughs about it in the "Chapter of Gradasso (Braggart)". Gradasso Berrettai was the dwarf of Cardinal Ippolito dei Medici, with whom Berni had gone on duty in 1532. Gradasso (what an ironic name!) "king of the pygmies," was from Norcia, and he was ungainly like no other, especially in the way of hopping, "which was not so much like: "a cricket, a cat, a dog, and a bitch". For such a personality the poet asks himself:

His genealogy who could say?
I find that he came out of one of those holes
Where at Norcia lives the Sibyl.
His father indeed castrated pigs
And he graduated as a maker of caps
So that he wouldn't live uselessly like a caterpillar amongst the leaves. (53)

Ah yes, a type of that sort must truly have been born in a cave!

Aretino, who
of all he spoke ill except for God,
which he excused himself by saying,
'I don't know him,'
barely skims over the subject in the "Second Day" of his *Reasoning* (1534-1536), in a risque narration.

Nanna tells of a woman who, in order to go to her lover, quarreled on purpose with her husband. She fled the house and left her clothes on the edge of a deep well, so that her relatives would believe she had drowned. After an intoxicating season of love, she returned to the house, with the help of a necromantic friar "who invoked the spirits and had ampules full of them." She told her mother and husband "of the way that she lived in the well; and let them understand that the 'sister of the Sibyl of Norcia' and the aunt of the fairy Morgana live there, pulling down the many willing to be seduced. But what do you know? The well gained such a reputation that a grid of iron was put over it and everyone who had a strange husband drank the water, which seemed to do them good. Thereafter all those who were about to get married came to show their devotion, praying to the fairy that she give them good fortune. And in one year more candles, more clothes, more undershirts and more wooden votive tablets were offered than there were around the sepulcher of the Holy Saint Lena da l'Olio of Bologna." (54)

Aretino, "anti-Christ of the century" as he was called by Doni, laughed at fairies and saints and certainly wasn't disposed to kneel before the Sibyl.

More inclined to believe in the necromantic arts and omens of the Sibilline mountains was that blockhead Cellini, whose father, hoping for a "male son," at birth called him exultantly: Welcome/Benvenuto!

In the recounting of his *Life*, in chapters 64-65 a "cleric" necromancer makes an appearance; a Sicilian priest, expert in the magical arts, in which Benvenuto ardently wanted to be instructed. On the invitation of the priest he went twice, with a few acquaintances, to the Colosseum to assist in the invocation of devils. This was done "with circles on the earth and with the most beautiful ceremonies", so that "the Colosseum was full," especially during

76

the second experience when they were taken with the most tremendous fear because "all the Colosseum burned and the fire came up behind them." So the same intrepid Benvenuto, author of the most pleasurable bragging in history "had as much fear as anyone," and "was scared to death" even though "one did one's best to show no fear and to demonstrate great courage" in particular to "a little virgin boy," a type of "medium," who from immeasurable fear gave out spontaneous noises with associated substances of foul odor, turning in flight in such mode the infinite legions of devils!

At any rate, the priest, satisfied with the experiment, asked the Florentine goldsmith "to accompany him to consecrate a book" with which he would be able to find "infinite riches" and "treasures, of which the earth is full."

But go where? And the priest answered him:

> "In less than a month we will go out on this enterprise, and that the place most suitable was in the mountains of Norcia. Although a master had consecrated such a book nearby at the place called the Abbey of Farfa, there had been some difficulties there, which they would not have in the mountains of Norcia; and that those peasants of Norcia are persons of faith, and have some practice in these things; they could give marvelous assistance in case of need."

Added Benvenuto:

> "This necromantic priest certainly had me very persuaded, so that I was gladly disposed to do such a thing, but I said that first I wanted to finish the medal that I was making for the Pope." (55)

Fortunately art absorbed him so much that it definitively distracted him from the deadly proposition.

The other bizarre Florentine genius, Anton Francesco Doni, imagined that the Lago di Pilato was the hell of the poets, watched carefully by the Sibyl. She would only permit visits to it under her guidance (56), as if to recall the episode in which Aeneas descended (to hell) in Avernus.

Doni writes:

> "he who wishes to see all the disgraces, all the reverses of fortune that you can possibly imagine and the tricks that ignorance has put in use, should read of this hell and note well all the torments of the poets; that would give him good warning, if he bears it all in mind." (57)

The Scholars of the 16ᵗʰ and 17ᵗʰ Centuries

These are the last glimmerings of the grand literature of the Sibilline legends–at times little more than traces. In the records that we have from various scholars at the end of the 16ᵗʰ and into the 17ᵗʰ century, the information, the reflections, and the scepticism often overwhelm the native born magic of the fairytale winding vivaciously through their drowsy pages. They are writers, nonetheless, who bear witness to how our legends became famous again in all Europe at the end of the 15ᵗʰ and into the 16ᵗʰ century.

A prime example is Abramo Oertel (1527-1598) also called the latinate "Oetelius," in his *Theatrum Orbis Terrarum.* (58) His geographical description is sometimes majestic: a mountain in the Appenines dominates the Marches region and at its highest summit lies that horrifying cave called the Grotto della Sibilla by the people. Up there, they imagine, are the Elysian fields ("campos elysios fingunt"). The local people dream that in this cave is a Sibyl who possesses a vast realm, spangled with magnificent regal palaces, sprinkled with delightful gardens, and inhabited by amorous girls, with an abundance of every type of pleasure.

This paradise could be enjoyed by all those who wanted to join the Sibyl, by passing through an open cave. After a year of rapture in the palace, the guests, if they desired, could return to the world, where they lived happily the rest of their lives protected by the Queen Sibyl. Oertel then records the tragic events of Daniele, observing that in Germany, the mountain of the Sibyl is called also "Frau Venus Berg," that is, the mountain of the Lady Venus.

The writing of G.A. Magini (1555-1616) has none of the magical and dreamy touches of Oertel's , but instead the disdain of the scholar distressed by the "rubbish" of the "liars" and of the "imposters." (59) Regarding the noted phenomena of the water of the lake, " the hapless common folk think that up there live demons who respond when called" and that there is "an immeasurable and horrible cave, popularly called the cavern of the Sibyl, of which the liars and imposters recite much nonsense; where the Norcians, seeing the frequent numbers of enchanters and evil doers who converge there, were compelled to break it up and to cover the cave well and to also put a prudent guard over the lake."

More than the Lago di Pilato with its "cacodaemones " (filthy demons), Paolo Merula (P. Von Merle), in his *Cosmographia Generalis* (60) published in 1621, dwells with quite a bit of pleasure on the enchanted grotto. He lingers over the loves that one savors to satiation, the realm "luculentum et spatiosum" (light and spacious) the retinue of "lascivientium" (lascivious) girls, the shining palaces, but also details the horrifying transformation of the Sibyl, her young women, and the guest lovers into serpents and "in teterrimis beluis"(hideous monsters): prior and necessary passage of all the youths who then want to immerse themselves in the dreamy delights of the senses.

By the 1600's, the Sibilline grotto was so well known in all Europe that Beyerlink discussing the locations of the Sibyls in his noted *Magnum Theatrum Vitae Humanae* (1678), didn't hesitate to assert that according to the most widely held opinion they live in the Piceno, in the Appenines, and described the celebrated cavern with Oertel as his faithful guide. (61)

In remembrance of our grotto there is one poem from about the middle of the 1500's and another from the first thirty years of the 1600's which offer something to read but little to delight.

The first, titled *Il Meschino e Il Guerino* was written perhaps around 1547 by Tullia D'Aragon, a Roman courtesan. It is little more than a versification of the work of the same name by Andrea da Barberino, notwithstanding that in the Preface it says that the work is inspired by an old Spanish romance. (62)

The second, by the title *Tito Vespasiano overo Gerusalemme Desolata,* was written by G.B. Lalli (1572-1623). As regards the Sibilline legends it is perhaps more lively, especially in the depiction of the harsh landscape. Here it describes how Vespasia, grandmother of Tito Vespasiano, arrives through unprecedented hardships with her little grandson at the Grotta della Sibilla:

> And Vittore already overcome and
> With much sweat the steep altitude defeated,
> Arrive at the cave, where in its deep
> Bowels the wise Woman listens.
> The horribly dark mouth opens
> Of that fearful Sibilline grotto
> Where the sun never enters nor pure air,
> But the shadowy horror perpetually darkens
> (Ch. II, verse 45-46). (63)

As Febo Allevi persuasively suggests (64), Parini recalls the most blood-curdling myths of the Sibilline Mountains when, in his *Mattino,* he describes the metamorphosis of the fairies into serpents:

> "It is rumored thus that on the fifth day the fairies
> see their immortal bodies already covered

with horrible scales, and in witness thereof they turn into serpents
crawling on the ground, making
arching coils, forceful and strong.
But the first sun reveals them as more beautiful than ever,
making the lovers blissful; and by turning their eyes
the earth and the sea bend to their wishes." (65)

It is truly the fable of the enchanted Grotta della Sibilla, rising to noble
literary heights through the prestigious pen of the "insubro" poet.

Perhaps it is not worth mentioning that later Goethe in *Faust* (II Act IV)
refers to our mountains when he describes the tragic death of Cecco d'Ascoli,
called the "necromancer of Norcia": "already the dead branches crackled and
raised tongues of fire...Great are the forces of the mountain; Up there nature
works with free immeasurable power." (66)

Following this the only written works concerning the Sibilline
Mountains are about botany and philology. One has to wait for our century
to find pleasure again in beautiful pages written by fine writers about the
enchanted fairytale.

The Contemporaries

At the beginning of the 1900's the Sibilline legends fired the imagination
of two dramatists, Aristide Sartorio and Domenico Tumiati. Aristide Sartorio
was inspired to write a work with the explicit title, *The Sibyl* (1922), "a figurative, dramatic poem" as Crocioni defined it. In four acts, it reevokes the
saga of Tannhäuser. The name of the protagonist is Lionello, who is briefly
mentioned in *Guerin Meschino*. He is the son of a king and leader of the
armed forces. One day he climbs to the Lago di Pilato along with his squire
and there he finds the necromancers intent on carrying out nefarious rites on
the occasion of Holy Week. A terrifying storm forces Lionello and the squire
to take refuge in the nearby Grotta della Sibilla. Here the desire arises in
them to explore the enchanted realm, notwithstanding the wise advice of a

hermit. Lionello passes the metal doors, jumps over a river of fire and finds himself in the seductive arms of the infernal enchantress.

On the eve of Good Friday, he comes to his senses when he sees the disgusting metamorphosis of the Sibyl and all her squalid court into snakes. He runs to the Pope, who, as we know, refuses him absolution. In the final grandiose scene, set in the Basilica of St. Peter, the Pope, seen with his crozier flowering in his hand, looks for the vanished knight in order to grant him pardon, but in vain. (67)

Some years earlier, Domenico Tumiati was inspired more directly by the adventures of Andrea da Barbarino's hero in his delicate *Dramatic Legend–Guerin Meschino* in three acts.(68)

Both narrative and descriptive prose draw inspiration from our legends. The exquisite Fabio Tombari recalled it to the artistic summit in his masterwork, the always delightful *Tutta Frusaglia*. Hear how much charm there is in this fairytale nourished by popular freshness:

> "The bailiff, that one from Filetti, said that in the bowels of the mountain, beyond a hen with chicks of gold, and a sow with piglets of gold, there is a sorceress who weaves day and night at a loom of gold.
> "And they don't go down to take it?"
> "They have tried. They went all the way into the belly of the Sibilla, but they couldn't. Neither with candles nor with torches!"
> "And why not?"
> "The wind of hell put out all the lights—and that was the end of it."

And further along:

> "It was there that he saw the book of commands, the book with which Cecco, the wizard of Ascoli, commanded the infernal spirits. But his shimmering goal lay beyond that."
> "If God gives me life"—he said— "if St. Antonio assists me and the mare bears me, at the cost of using up this little bit of breath that remains to me, on May 6, I want to arrive where Il Meschino

arrived. To cross the Sibillines, to arrive finally at Norcia, where there is still the breed of black piglets."(69)

While still living in the mythical memory of Il Meschino, the beautiful fairytale spreads in popular new directions and takes on the flavor of poetry.

The elegant and delicate Titta Rosa paid more attention to the horrible landscape of the Sibillincs than to the legend. In a brilliant article, written in1941 following a tempest of wind and rain which surprised him during his visit to these alpine places, he said:

> "While we were taking the return route, the Sibyl, mindful of her own repute, and so as not to prove Nicolo Peranzoni wrong, had already amassed over our heads black clouds, leaden and immense. In a few minutes the beautiful verdant high plateau changed color, became ashen, livid, fearsome. A witches' Sabbath fell on the earth, and immediately water began to beat down in windy torrents, in cascades, with a truly diabolical force. The wind twisted the trees frighteningly, our cars swerved on the descending road; it seemed that a blast of wind only a bit stronger would be enough to sweep them away like bugs, down into some wide open abyss. Dreadful lightening flashed in the black mass of the clouds with a gaiety that made us shiver. It thundered with an acute rumbling, like a grand orchestra. The Valkyries, on horses of clouds, stormed the earth. Who could it be making all this uproar, if not the Sibyl?"

In sum, a landscape and a sky worthy of their infernal fame, a symphonic variation on the tempest of squalls in the "vein of wind" within the choked and dark corridors of the grotto described by Antoine De La Sale. But Titta Rosa is too perceptive not to notice the Sibilline myth running mysteriously within those gorges flayed by wind and bombarded by rain:

> "It is certain, even when only looking at them from a distance, that a spirit of legend stirs in these mountains. The imagination of the

shepherds, lit and stimulated by memories of ancient myths and renewed later by the breath of Christianity, gave rise to the beautiful legend even if it didn't originate it". (70)

Piovene, however, preferred to remember the meadows of the Monte della Sibilla, iridescent with flowers, the blue mountains of a rare beauty, perhaps the most marvelous of Central Italy:

"In the Sibillines is the Grotta della Sibilla and there the legend of Guerin Meschino was born. They are still fabulous today for their stupendous springtime flowering, the most beautiful in Italy, they tell me, and unknown to many because of the isolation in which they persistently remain". (71)

And do you want to leave Colsalvatico out of the annals of the Sibillines? Certainly not! With a blast of phosphorescent images he describes the enchanted landscapes of our mountains, evoking the perennial myths:

"The hills gallop toward the transparence of the Appenines, on which a clear sky rests, and the eagle, with ample and calm circles, marks his possession. One makes out the bright crown of the sorceress Sibyl, the enchantress of Guerin Meschino, who fascinated the philosophers of Europe and inspired Heine and Wagner. The sorceress Sibyl is a daily reality; Guerin Meschino is the first person you meet or the first you hear mentioned. The fountain at which you quench your thirst carries his name, the roads where you travel are marked by the agile feet of the fairies still trembling from dancing with the shepherds, before the dawn when they would be changed into the cloven hooves of goats".

And further along, with a sublime figurative impulse he continues:

"Far off Vettore is like a reference point, it goes ever higher to penetrate the sky. To fill your hands with stars all you have to do is climb up there; if you found yourself there you could rise on your tiptoes and with your finger press a star like a button, and who knows if the world of the Sorceress wouldn't open up... The voice of the rivers grows distant, the trees spread out in the shade; the Sibillines are the last to plunge into the dark, silhouetting their mass up above the shadows which rise up from the ravines. Now Monte Sibilla is full of fairies, ready to descend at the order of the enchantress Sorceress. She has lost connection with the valleys; the cries of the children don't touch her; she is only in contact with the abyss. She waits on high in her fairytale realm, and rules the dreams of the valley. All night long she preserves her mystery; at first light she becomes an unadorned and inaccessible mountain again, for the profane who don't know how to dream with their eyes open". (72)

There would also be two unpublished poems in dialect by another Marchigiano, Enrico Ricciardi of Sarnano, inspired by the events of Guerin Meschino and by the legends of the grotto, but still waiting the generous editor who will print them.(73)

Finally we remember Furio Jesi, who in a lively journalistic report for *Storia Illustrata,* after having retraced the way of Il Meschino, has left us a flavorful description of the Sibillines and of their incandescent fables. (74)

Nor have we forgotten the contemporary artists of the Sibyl. We call to mind the great Marchigiano sculptor, Pericle Fazzini, who has given us the gift of that supreme sculpture which is the Sibyl personified, a masterwork of seductive forms, mobile and absorbed in the harmony of space.

CHAPTER VI

THE PHILOLOGISTS

After the poets and the prose writers come the philologists, in a cultural stage characterized by positive science. From the close of the 19th century and up until today, they turn to the Sibilline legends with the attitude of cultured and subtle investigators.

By this time the myth had evaporated forever. Nevertheless there was still an artist, the greatest, to reanimate the ashes of the ancient Sibilline legends — Wagner.

In 1841 in Paris, Wagner was charmed by the fabulous story of Tannhäuser, the German knight who throws himself away on perpetual adventures until he disappears into a paradisaical realm, given to him by means of infernal witchcraft. Of this was born a sovereign musical work, entitled appropriately *"Tannhäuser"*, put on for the first time in Dresden in 1841 and later also in Paris in 1861. (75)

Paris, Rajna, and Other "Masters"

It was then that Gaston Paris, learned scholar of romantic literature, stimulated by the Wagnerian opera, became interested in Tannhäuser. This led by reflex to the legends of the Sibyl, considered by many the origin of the myth of the German knight.

In 1872, after some studies, he confided the overall purpose of his investigations in substance to one of the most distinguished Italian philologists. Alessandro D'Ancona had to disappoint Paris by telling him that just the previous year, in 1871, Alfred Reumont had "stolen the march" on the fascinating argument, dealing with it at a conference at the Colombaria of Florence. (76)

By now the spark of the "inflammable" legend had been cast and the incendiary philologist did not delay in flaring up. Later Paris consulted another "boss" of Italian critical positivism, Pio Rajna, with whom he began a series of historical-philological surveys, necessitating harsh and embittering excursions to the Sibilline Mountains.

Meanwhile other celebrated "masters" threw themselves into the fray with erudite studies of real interest. Graf, in an essay of 1889, published the original texts of P. Bersuire and Fra Bernardino da Foligno, fundamental to the legend of the Lago di Pilato. (77) Torraca took part in completing the catalog of literary sources relative to the two legends. (78) Neri, the founder of the *Collezione Classici Italiani* UTET, discussed with rare competence the complex events of the myth of the Sibyl in Italy. (79)

And of course there is the controversy over the origin of the legend of Tannhäuser, which burns with unusual intensity. Consequently, the authoritative participation of various foreign scholars is recorded: the Finnish Werner Söderhjelm (80), the Swiss Heinrich Dübi, who drew attention to the text of F. Hemmerlin (81), and above all the Belgian, Fernand Desonay. He dedicated years of attentive research to the Sibilline myths, with particular interest in De La Sale, whose critical edition of *Le Paradis de la Reine Sibylle* he edited, prefacing it with a scholarly "Introduction". (82)

The Local Scholars

Following the example of the "greats," the scholars of the Marches and of Umbria, for love of their birthplace, also contributed valuable studies to the investigation of the legends. Among them stands out: Speranza, who advanced hypotheses on the identification of the Sibyl (83), Crocioni, who collected popular legends and related bibliography of the Sibilline myths (84), Vittori, who illustrated the history of Montemonaco and of its enchanted mountains (85), Amadio, who tirelessly investigated the place names of the Marches including the Sibilline region (86), and Paolucci, who defended a dense and merit-worthy graduate dissertation on the topic, reproducing in the appendix virtually all of the ancient and modern documents relative to the grotto and the lake. (87) There is Falzetti, generous and intelligent collaborator with Desonay and author of valuable essays as well as the Italian translation of the *Paradis* by De La Sale (88), Fabi who also published new documents illustrating the history and legends of the zone of the Sibillines (89), and the tireless Febo Allevi with a very learned study, fundamental to our discussion (90), etc...

But that doesn't silence the authoritative voices of the foreigners. The German W. Pabst magisterially summarized the results of the criticism on the subject matter in a dense and well documented essay. (91) Another very acute study was written by the Scandinavian Marjatta Wis. (92)

Of the numerous scholars who interested themselves in our legends, we have only mentioned the "fixed stars," without naming the "planets," which have turned and still turn around them, reciprocating theses and ideas. It would be arduous and boring to refer to all of them, a matter of bibliography which branches out infinitely, bottomless like the Lago di Pilato. (93)

The Nodal Points of the Legends: The Myth of Tannhäuser

It is useful, however, to recall the nodal points of their discussions and polemics. These, in our opinion, when stripped of many problematic complexities, can be summarized as two: the origin of the myth of Tannhäuser with the attached question of the Mountain of Venus, and the origin of the tradition of the Sibyl in our mountains.

But what does the Teutonic Tannhäuser have to do with the Piceno Sibillines? Tannhäuser and the Sibillines intersect where the events of his tale seem to reflect those of the Guerin Meschino of Andrea Barbarino, and then again of the German knight of A. De La Sale, and further, in the Simplicianus of F. Hemmerlin and Daniele of Oertel.

Tannhäuser, a "minnesänger", adventurer/soldier of fortune, was born around 1205 of a noble family in Salzburg and died around 1268. As a poet he left few traces, as an adventurer many. He was enamored of the "good life", of song and dance, inspired by 'courtly love' in a tone now realistic, now ironic. It seems that he participated in the Crusade of 1228.

Later, his wealth lost, he wandered from court to court and finally disappeared mysteriously. After an undefined span of time, the legend began to envelop him in its vaporous and fleeting nimbus. It is fabled that Tannhäuser had penetrated into the Mountain of Venus, living amongst the lively passions in a world of witchcraft, with the goddess. Then, repenting his sins, he went to Rome to ask for pardon from Pope Urbano II. The Pope would not give him absolution, telling him that, just as his crozier couldn't flower, so he could not absolve Tannhäuser. The knight, made desperate and gloomy by lacerating remorse, decided to plunge back again into the seductive arms of Venus, forever. In the meantime, after three days, the crozier of the Pope flowered like a sprig in spring and in vain the Pope ordered a search for Tannhäuser.

But this is the legend of the German knight told by A. De La Sale and similar to that of Simplicianus by F. Hemmerlin, of Daniele of Oertel, and then "in nuce" in Guerin Meschino! And so all those persons could be identified with Tannhäuser!

The scholars realized the connection, and among the first to do so was Gaston Paris. However, in Germany the myth of Tannhäuser created a miraculous flowering of poems and other writings, especially in the 15th-16th centuries and up until the apex of the sublime songs of Wagner. Therefore the German scholars wanted to claim the German origination of the myth itself, without humiliating "national" tributes to the Sibilline myth, while the scholars of other nations, above all the French (naturally!), wanted to refute this German origination. In fact the analogies, especially with the knight of *Paradis* are undeniable and clear. It is also undeniable that the first report of Tannhäuser in the realm of Venus–which one reads in the poem *Die Möhrin* by H. Von Sachsenhelm–dates back only to 1453, a good forty-four years after *Guerin Meschino* and thirty-three years after *Paradis* by A. De La Sale.

The scholars line up in battle on various fronts: Paris, Rajna, Desonay, Dübi, and Wis, even with the inevitable interpretive shadings, were convinced that the legend of Tannhäuser was linked to Guerino and to the "cavalier" of De La Sale, and that it passes therefore through the Sibilline Mountains. Above all, Dübi is especially persuasive. He perceives in the writing of Hemmerlin the "trait-d'union" between the Sibilline legend and the German legend of Tannhäuser: the first could have emigrated to the mountains of Lucerne through the mediation of pilgrims from Rome who traveled north, and from there it could have ended up in Germany.

Other scholars, however, like Schmidt, Elster, Reuschel, and Meyer, lay claim to the German "nationality"of both the myth of Tannhäuser and of Venusberg. Others like Kluge and Plaff, after Grimm, are somewhat more inclined to compromise, seeming disposed to consider that the myth of Venusberg, tacked on to the German legend of the cursed knight, could have had an independent life in Italy.

In the end, Desonay observed, one returns to the hypothesis of Söderhjelm. He had thought of a kind of fusion, realized by A. De La Sale, of two distinct themes: the Italian myth of a mountain of love and the German legend of Tannhäuser in the cavern of Venus.

Desonay also points out the thesis of the distinguished folklorist Golther, who ended up proposing again the singular theory of Grässe, that is: the legends could have germinated from a substrate of remote traditions, such as the mythical loves of an elf with a human being.

The studies of Remy and above all of Barto reawakened the problem of the origin of our legend. Both of them were favorable in substance to the German thesis. Remy imagines an antique pagan myth of celtic tradition, combined with a lost Christian motive, at the base of the legend. Barto thinks that the enigma of Tannhäuser and Venusberg is intimately bound up with the myth of the Grail.

There were also those who sought the prehistory of Tannhäuser in oriental sources, like Abel, or in the always vital streams of classical and medieval literature, which gelled in the sad legend of Guerino, as Pabst supposes. (94)

But–as Wis also confirms–it is difficult to ignore the derivation of the myth of Tannhäuser from the literature of the Sibilline grotto, since doing so denies analogies of content and the recognition of chronological priority. One can't forget that as early as around 1487, Giovanni Delle Piatte already speaks of Tannhäuser in the Grotta della Sibilla.

Implicitly bound up with the problem of the Tannhäuser myth is the problem of Venusberg. One knows that the Mountain of the Sibyl is also called the Mountain of Venus, to indicate the spiritual connotations of its bewitching inhabitant. But why the Mountain of Venus, Venusberg?

Allevi thinks that on the fateful mountain, a temple was raised in classical antiquity dedicated to Cybele or to Cupra or to Venus; all goddesses with clear aphrodisiacal characteristics. At this temple pagan priests could have "convened to give vent to their frenzies". (95) Thus it was called Venusberg because of the temple dedicated to Venus.

But the first explicit reports of a Venusberg in the Sibillines appear in the writing of Felix Hemmerlin, around 1444-1450. German knights like Arnolfo di Harff ask news of it, and G. Delle Piatte speaks implicitly of it when he describes the "Lady Venus". In consequence one can think, as for example Neri did, that the creation of Venusberg could be attributed to the "Germanic imagination". Wis links our mountain to that of Pafo, on the island of Cyprus, upon which arose a temple of Aphrodite. She observes, however, that the connection is not verified in classical antiquity (even if the sanctuary of Venus on the hill of Ancona could be thought an eloquent example of such a cult to the goddess in the Piceno region) but in the Middle Ages, by the mediation of pilgrims, crusaders, and Germans, all wanderers along the Via Flaminia. (96)

What's more, the appearance of the myth of Venusberg signals the deformation of the ancient figure of the Sibyl. At one time a wise and beneficial seer, even welcomed in the Christian culture amongst the prophetic announcers of the advent of the Messiah, she becomes the diabolical creator of a realm of infernal lasciviousness.

Already, in *Guerin Meschino,* one witnesses this sad metamorphosis. The "virgin" Sibyl, aspiring to receive in herself the miracle of the incarnation of the Son of God, stirred with prideful wrath when the Virgin Mary was selected in her place. Despairing, she shut herself up in the impervious Sibilline rocks. From inaccessible virgin she became an impious and greedy seductress (97), lost in immediate desires, as has already been plainly revealed in the tales of Andrea da Barbarino, Antoine De La Sale, and Felix Hemmerlin.

A Sibyl, then, transformed into Venus.(98)

And here we could note that in the Santuario dell'Ambro the painter Martino Bonfini between 1610 and 1611 portrayed the Cumaen Sibyl in the flourishing form of a young woman, in which could be read secret feminine seductiveness with its lively and thriving aspect. She stands in striking contrast to the rather withered forms of the other Sibyls painted here, who were also considered prophetesses of the future Christian era. The artist, in his pictoral cycle of the Madonna in a sanctuary situated practically at the feet of the famous Sibilline grotto, apparently wanted to embody in the figure of the Cumaen Sibyl, linked to the legend of the nearby mountains, the theme of prophecy (expressed in her book of predictions), as much as the theme of voluptuousness (hinted at in the form of a woman of enchanting description.)

The Origin of the Myth of the Sibyl

But how did the cult of the Sibyl ascend to such a high altitude? Here is the second core problem of the legend which, under a rigorously logical outline, could also be the first.

The old Italian writers, from Andrea da Barbarino (who put in the mouth of the Fairy these words: "The Trojan leader Aeneas goes with me through all of hell".) to Trissino, Peranzoni, Lalli, etc., immediately identified our Sibyl with that of Cumae. According to them she had been exiled to the frozen Umbrian/Marchigiani Appenines at the advent of Christianity and stripped of her ancient prestige.

But Antoine De La Sale speaks of a "false" Sibyl, without history.(99) Nevertheless the tradition continued to identify the Cumaen Sibyl with ours, until with the advent of modern philology, the knot came to the comb and illustrious minds wearied themselves almost in vain untangling it.

Speranza, at the dawning of our century, seemingly agreed to the traditional thesis without particular apprehensions (100), but Paris and Rajna wanted to delve deeper to track down the evidentiary signs of a high medieval or even premedieval Sibyl. They believed they had found the winning card in the reference by De La Sale to certain "seats" carved in the grotto. The only thing is that not even the faintest surviving traces, from the archeological point of view, could confirm the hypothesis. The secret doubt over the veracity of the account of Antoine remains and broke into pieces the last resistance to the traditional thesis.(101)

Those seats could have revealed the existence of ancient rites in the cave, similar to those that are rendered to the goddess Cybele in Phrygia. Desonay was moved to this supposition, and through acute and elegant conjectures linking them, affirmed that Cybele, the Great Mother of Anatolia, at the epoch of her passage from Pessinunte to Rome (around 240 A.D.) also began to have a cult in the Sibilline Mountains. Evidence of that could be the similarities of the landscapes with their curative waters and springs, and dense woods, and the Monte della Sibilla with its crest, resembling a statue of the crowned goddess Cybele. (102)

But Pabst is not of the same opinion as Desonay, above all because between the cult of the goddess Cybele of the 3rd century A.D. and the legend of Il Meschino is a chasm of time mute with the silence of stone.

Allevi, however, shared the thesis of the Belgian Desonay and strove to produce new archeological evidence and to develop other conjectures about the cult of the goddesses Cybele, Cupra, and Venus in the Piceno region, and, by reflection in the Appenine grotto. He proposed again the indeed difficult hypothesis, already advanced by others, according to which "Sibilla" is etymologically derived from "Cybele."(103) The mass of references is truly impressive, because the distinguished scholar didn't leave out any document which could assist his learned inquiry. His logical reasoning is persuasive only as long as it takes a wide view to demonstrate the presence of the cult of Cybele, of Cupra, and of Venus, in ancient Piceno. It unravels, however, and breaks down when it tries to show that the Sibilline Grotto in that distant time was one of the cult's centers. The illustrious scholar was consequently obliged to proceed by conjecture, for the simple reason that it was impossible to produce a single document that "cuts the head from the bull".

Amadio seems disposed to admit an ancient cultic presence in the Sibilline grotto; he makes reference, besides Cybele, to Cupra, whose cult was very widespread in ancient Piceno. (104) Falzetti, by means of a discussion rich in scholarly ramifications, ventures to set up a difficult link between the Etruscan goddess Nortia, the goddess Fortuna, and the Sibyl of our mountains.

Paolucci was strongly opposed to the conjecture of an ancient cult of Cybele in the Sibilline grotto. By way of an intricate argument he wanted to "point out the incongruence of a thesis which would claim to illuminate the Sibyl, misunderstood in the light of the Phrygian divinity, while ending up by creating a Cybele linked with difficulty to the true Appenine Sibyl, of whom Desonay, after many more or less scholarly arguments, does not know how to give us any sort of explanation". Instead, the opinion of Paolucci is as follows: the Sibyl of Montemonaco was born from the popular imagination. Spontaneously, without ties to historic or scholarly characters, it placed the prophetess on the summit of the Piceno mountains, perhaps in the same century in which the legend of Pilate flowered. (105)

But how can this proposition be unequivocably demonstrated?

All the scholars proceed precariously on the fine razor edge of supposition, supported neither by sufficient written sources from Roman or early Christian and Medieval eras, nor by verifiable archeological finds.

One asks spontaneously: please mister philologists, a document of identity! But who could offer it?

Perhaps it's better this way. The legend can continue to live in an indefinable historical dimension, preserving the vapors characteristic of the mysterious fairytale. Better too, if no one can think that it either sprouted one morning from nothing or that it flowered as if by a magic charm from the pen of the author of *Guerino* without a preexisting popular voice.

Two representations of Guerin Meschino, taken from ancient prints and reproduced in *Storia Illustrata,* (1964-65). With the stirring and breezy adventures of Il Meschino, the legends of the grotto rose into the heights of literary nobility and became famous throughout Europe.

The Appenine Sibyl, represented in classical garments following the Virgilian tradition, all intent on deciphering the future in the reading of "Sibilline" texts (from *Storia Illustrata*). She was seen in this interpretive light by Italian authors, amongst them Trissino, who said of her "most ancient of years and wisdom."

Signatures (with devices) of Antoine De La Sale, Her Hans Wan Bamborg (intravit) and Thomin De Pons or De Pous. The first is carved directly into the rock and the other two transcribed from the walls of the grotto by De La Sale, who climbed up there in May 1420

.

100

The Cumaean Sibyl painted by Martino Bonfini (1610-11) on the walls of the Sanctuary of the Ambro. The figure appears to combine the classical characteristics of the prophetess, indicated by the writings at the bottom, and the characteristics of theenchanting inhabitant of the grotto, alluding to her voluptuous feminine form.

Detail of the mouth of the grotto, where one can make out, high up, some monogrammatic letters and an arabic numeral (1378), brought to light by the excavations of 1953.

Two views of the entrance of the Grotto of the Sibyl, which, after the most recent and sporadic tests, is in a pitiful state and waits to be fully explored.

CHAPTER VII

THE EXCAVATIONS AT THE GROTTO OF THE SIBYL

Gaston Paris and Pio Rajna–it is said–based their theory of a pre-medieval cult in the grotto on the "seats" carved inside, as described by A. De La Sale. But first those seats must be found. Thus they proposed to visit the grotto for archeological verification of this key information.(106)

The First Scientific Excursions of Rajna

So it was that on June 23,1897 the first scientific excursion of modern times to the fateful grotto took place. But the Mountain of the Sibyl, just like in the legend, imposed its terrible veto with an impenetrable mass of fog and the threat of storms. The less intrepid Gaston stopped at Norcia. Pio, however, was swallowed up by the wet dense blanket, groping to the brink of the precipices within the inextricable woods, towards the enchanted cave. His guide took them on the wrong path. After unprecedented difficulties Pio finally reached the cave, only to impotently contemplate a huge boulder which choked the throat of the moribund grotto. After little more than a glance, he turned back towards Norcia. But his guide lost the way again, and led the philologist/alpinist roundabout through the harsh blood- red rocks of Monte Sibilla.

The following August, Rajna tried the undertaking again. It was a happier excursion, but again disappointing because the archeological survey lacked results. At the end of the same month he went up there a third time, with the idea of gathering useful information from the mountain people.

Meanwhile he told his friend Gaston, who had returned to comfortable Paris, about his mishaps and his meager results in a copious series of letters. Rajna had seen for himself that the mouth of the underground passage was irremediably strangled with detritus and rocks, and he sought to investigate the causes, reconstructing the events. He knew that deluded treasure hunters, accompanied by a priest armed with an aspergill, had forced the entrance. The opening had been guarded in the past, as the first documents record, and more than once it was closed by the authority of Norcia, determined to avoid foolish manifestations of superstition and gullibility.

A shepherd and a certain Zeffirino told Rajna that they had ventured into the interior of the grotto between 1860 and 1870, penetrating between 200 and 300 meters. But Rajna was too sensible to give credit to such tales that ran nimbly to the edge of the fairytale. He had to give credence, instead, to his disappointed eyes, which rested mournfully on the entrance of the grotto, now suffocated, strangled by the crushed stones of landslides lying together with mute and solemn boulders like petrified guards at the door of the realm of the Sibyl.

To the work of man, who knows how to tamper with everything, time adds the gloomy violence of nature. Earthquakes, so frequent in the Sibillines even today, had broken into pieces, with sudden slashes and irresistible shrugs, the precipitous back of the mountain.

Even before Rajna, in 1885, G.B. Miliani had clearly seen the pitiful state of the grotto, which he recognized under "a cloud of rubble". (107) In August of 1889 a party of CAI members from Ascoli Piceno had sought in vain to put it right. After trying useless improvements to the asphyxiated hole, they had no better idea than the dismal one of leaving a gravestone in memory of the visit, placed, into the bargain, on that part of the rock which still preserved ancient and modern writing.(108)

Only many years after the excursion of Rajna was another scientific expedition possible, carried out by the young and industrious Falzetti and some of his friends in 1920. However, they had to satisfy themselves with discovering the enchanted underground passage only by means of a shepherd boy sliding down it feet first.

Meanwhile a "Committee for the excavations in the grotto of the Monte Sibilla" was formed at Montemonaco, with a plan of work drawn up by Dr. Mario Monti Guarnieri. According to this plan every judgement regarding the existence of an ample gallery beyond the obstructed entrance of the grotto was considered groundless as long as the thick detritus had not been removed from the entrance "below some meters where one enters badly and crookedly". (109)

Some years later the Committee enlarged itself and assumed the denomination of "Roman-Umbrian-Marchigiano", enriching itself with the prestigious support of Gaston Paris, Pio Rajna (honorary president), Domenico Falzetti (effective president), and later of Ferdinand Desonay.

In August 1925 they took up the archeological survey with the best intentions in the world, under the enthusiastic guidance of Falzetti. Would this finally be it?

First result: they learned that between 1922 and 1924 some superstitious fanatics, attracted again by the mirage of treasure, had made a mess of everything at the mouth of the grotto. In the beginning of Falzetti's expedition it was not even possible to find the shaft, which had already been located in August 1920. But the dedicated explorers, guided by the writing of A. De La Sale, dug and dug, until a surprise appeared: a square stone, in the form of an architrave horizontally placed with its ends on two stone posts in vertical positions.

Well then? Nothing less than a fresh burst of enthusiasm!

The works were stopped in 1925. Falzetti had to run back to Rome to ask for help from the "idol" of Italian philology, Pio Rajna, who had become a senator under the regime and therefore "powerful," as they say. And in fact, by the intercession of the "idol," the "management of the excavation" through divisional head Count Pellati, entrusted professor Moretti, superintendent of antiquities for the Marches, to carry out archeological tests at the Grotta della Sibilla.

The regime had moved and therefore something, "prophetically," could come to light! The diligent Moretti "was confident of being able to remove all of the material caved in over time from the ancient ground, and to penetrate into another cavity." (110)

But nothing doing! The Sibyl again gave her veto, to the regime as well, and did not grant a passport even to one of her most devoted worshipers. Desonay, in August 1929, attempted an archeological adventure at the entrance of the grotto all by himself, with much poetic enthusiasm but no practical results.

The following year Desonay, along with Falzetti and other enthusiasts, took the road to the impenetrable grotto again, but the Sibyl, writes Falzetti, "covered them with ridicule." (111) After they had removed load after load of rubble from the jammed mouth of the cavern, desiring at any cost to explore the depth of the passageway, they tried to plumb the belly with a cord weighted with a stone. The first stone, too small, buried itself in the sides and didn't pull down the cord: the second, too big, didn't go into the narrow opening...

But let us listen to the actual voice of Desonay, who evokes his fascinating excursions with rare freshness:

> "On the trail of the traveler of the 1400's (=A. De La Sale), I wanted to make the mysterious trip to the Sibilla again. Twice. The first time in 1929. August 26 I contemplated the play of the fog on the cliffs on the Appenines.
>
> I had in my pocket the text of Antoine De La Sale: I wanted to examine all of the topographic indications of the manuscript. And there we finally were before the "crown." And then there was the grotto (...).
>
> To return to my first visit, there was nothing extraordinary. The grotto; little more than a hole in the mountain. At the entrance, on the surface of the rock, some worn traces of engraved letters. The most important shaft obstructed. The paradise hidden...
>
> But the next year during my stay in Montemonaco, I had an oppor-

tunity to make a second, more fruitful visit to the grotto with the
Roman-Umbrian-Marchigiano Committee for the Sibilla between
August 15 and 18, 1930. Recent work there had changed its appearance: the opening of the shaft had disappeared: one saw a noteworthy ditch at the bottom of which were various large stones. For the
amount of work completed, the unknown excavators could have
achieved something good if instead of following a blind alley, they
had followed the track of the old shaft with more confidence .
A large stone, obstructing the entrance and said to have been rolled
there by shepherds, was completely bare, not the appearance of nor-
mal detritus. The group began to remove the earth around the stone;
and very soon, at the lowest point on the left, the correct way was
found. After an hour an opening about 2 meters deep was dug and
an empty space was revealed. I, myself, with the help of a wind-
proof torch, saw a void in the bottom of the excavation.
Furthermore, one member of the committee felt a light current of air
coming from the inside." (112)

At this point the ardent explorers tried an "enema" in the dark intestines
of the grotto with a mock heroic system involving a stone tied to a cord, as
has been mentioned. And then "however reluctantly" they had to "retake the
road of return."

Colsalvatico, Lippi-Boncampi and the Excavations of 1953

Perhaps that stone remained there up through the Second World War,
when a happy storyteller and poet of the Marches, Tullio Colsalvatico, tried
the bewitched undertaking again. But I think that for the aristocratic and elegant Tullio, the poetic and narrative labors turned out more happily than the
archeological ones at the Grotta della Sibilla. On the other hand Lippi-
Boncampi , who climbed up there for an on-the-spot investigation in August
1946, said that the archeological poet (perhaps unique) "had put in evidence
some steps"(113) interpreted as corresponding to the "seats" of A. De La Sale.

Colsalvatico–as he told us personally with relish–passed long days of work in the full heat of the summer. He went up to the grotto taking a burro laden with tools and provisions. Then the hard work began, bent in the enigmatic grotto with the face of a sphinx, while the robust sun scorched his uncovered head. Further down in the valley, hunters shot deafening rounds in the mountain wilderness, making some believe that the grotto had collapsed under bursts of dynamite. When he descended to the village, the mountaineers, who called him the "sorcerer", with mysterious accents asked him astonished questions about his wizardly undertakings.

But the Sibyl, jealous and implacable, entrusted her friend the sun to burn the archeological enthusiasm out of the tireless poet. So as not to risk a serious sunstroke, he was forced to stop the enterprise–launched but not completed.

As for Lippi-Boncampi, the good geologist gave a heavy "scientific" blow to the Sibilline fable, announcing that according to his orographic (the study of the physical geography of mountains and mountain ranges) survey, nothing justified the belief in the existence of a spacious cave beyond the underground passage of the grotto, or of a subterranean passage between it and Foce.

But perhaps it was the enchantress Sibyl who hid her secret recesses from the presumptions of Science! Because of this the devotees of poetry continue to dream of a cave of the Fairy, vast and meandering. And the unshakable Desonay continued to go up there, as if to a sanctuary of fairytale and culture.

On February 1953, at the Accademia Belgica of Rome, Desonay gave a brilliant lecture on the annals and mysteries of the Sibilline grotto. He repeated it the next day at the Circolo Marchigiano, arousing an explosion of enthusiasm and bold proposals to try the archeological adventure at the enchanted cavern again the next summer.

And so in July 1953, Desonay, in the front line with Falzetti and Giovanni Annibaldi, (superintendent of antiquities in the Marches and guide of the expedition), along with another seventeen volunteers including four workers armed with pickaxes, climbed up to the grotto of the Queen Sibyl as if in a liturgical procession.

Also with them was a diviner, Emidio Santanche, who–miraculously!—felt the "nervous" divining rod leap between his hydromantic hands: the empty immense belly underneath responded to his diviners call. His staff twisted like someone possessed undergoing an exorcism and indicated a void to the left of the entrance, where backfill was piled.

Following the twitching diviners rod the pickaxes found the going heavy and impassable. And here was the first surprise: the former underground passages had disappeared! A sign that the Sibyl had withdrawn with her realm into the viscera of the earth, or more probably that a large vault had crumbled with the facade of the entrance, dragging down an immense pile of detritus...

The works proceeded at a quickened pace. The committee passed the night up there, under a mantle of infinite stars. Desonay and Annibaldi slept in the same tent, like two ancient Roman junior officers in a military camp. And like a battle camp, Desonay sent "war bulletins" on the excavations to a Belgian newspaper "Le Soir," non-stop from August 27 to September 2, 1953. But the hourglass of the 250,000 lire subsidy for the excavations let fall, grain by grain, all the meager monetary reserve; it was necessary, therefore, to cut corners.

Some Archeological Results

The rubble was cleared feverishly from the blocked mouth of the grotto, and everything of recent manufacture was demolished, starting with the vainglorious headstone of the CAI. Finally, some monogrammatic letters and an Arabic numeral came to light, interpreted by Falzetti as 1378.

Here were the unequivocal signs of a distant presence and of an ancient fable. These were affirmed by the finding of a piece of French money from the 16th century, obtained in a dig almost immediately following (still in July 1953), during which a horizontal subterranean passage also seemed to appear, in accordance with the description of A. De La Sale. (114) To explore it further, buttressing work was needed for the safety of the workers.

But what would the inaccessible bosom of the grotto be like? Would this now really be the enchanted grotto?

The answers are still unknown because the works of excavation ended here. The other visits of Desonay to the grotto, up until August 1956, were melancholy pilgrimages to the humiliated bones of the palace of an ancient and fabulous sovereign.

After so many hardships and hopes, what a bitter taste in the mouth!

But the enthusiasts of the Sibilline myths did not give up. After the appearance of the first edition of this booklet, Dante Cecchi, of the University of Macerata, wanted to rekindle the dying embers of the ancient hope. In a substantial article written following one of his excursions to the Monte della Sibilla, he thoroughly summarized the literary and archeological data relative to the grotto, asking, "Well then, does the Grotta della Sibilla (or better said, any grotto at all) exist or not? And are the legends all purely fiction?" He refers then to valuable and recent evidence about the cavern:

> "Andrea da Barbarino and Antoine De La Sale, who lived 550 years ago, spoke of water courses and cascades in the viscera of the Sibyl. But Father Maurizio Pierantoni, Rector of the Sanctuary of the Madonna of the Ambro, told me about Francesco Fermani, an eighty year old shepherd, who actually lived in Castel Sant'Angelo sul Nera. Fermani told him that when he was a boy of 13 or 14 (therefore at the beginning of this century), he had pastured his flock above Isola San Biagio just below the summit of the Monte della Sibilla. With some friends (because he was afraid to do it by himself), they entered the grotto. After passing through a kind of atrium, they descended into a cavity, where he heard the sound of water and saw a deep chasm into which he and his friends threw stones in order to hear them ricochet through the cavern as they fell and were lost in the abyss. What value do we want to give and can we give, to this testimony?"

Therefore Cecchi launched an appeal to the CAI of Macerata and to the townships of the Sibillines:

"Why doesn't the local section of the CAI of Macerata (and the "notables") along with other centers (I think above all of Amandola, a nearby town) try an organized campaign of inquiry? We have assisted in the opening of the system of caves in the Valley of Esino, of Frasassi and Genga; but the legends about the Grotta della Sibilla couldn't have been born by themselves (...) Today science provides instruments perfected for plumbing depths and subterranean prospecting. Why not try this?"(115)

Then in a learned and lively lecture in the Sala della Eneide at the Palazzo Buonaccorsi in Macerata on the November 21st 1974, Cecchi spoke to the public on the following theme: "The Monte della Sibilla–Legend and Reality."

Meanwhile the CAI of Macerata had been roused by the first appeal on November 14 1974, responding with the following communique:

"After a thorough study of the geological and hydrological probability of the existence of an underground complex, the board of directors of the speleological group of the CAI of Macerata has decided to dedicate a great part of their explorative activity to systematic research into the Grotta dell Sibilla.
Taking account of the interest which this grotto presents from the historical-mythological point of view, along with an eventual touristic interest, and considering above all that it could offer an underground complex of noteworthy importance, the speleological group of the CAI of Macerata, with great zeal and with all the means at its disposal, assisted by the members Drs. Giuliano Mainini and Corsalini Mario, and by the other groups of the CAI such as the rock climbing group and the school of alpine skiing, "Alti Sibillini", dedicate themselves to the exploration of such zone

without leaving anything untried and with the hope that the works
are crowned with success". (116)

Will these fresh and hopeful initiatives lead to positive results? Will the
lady of the enchanted palace grant an audience to the worshipers of her passionate myths? Or will she envelope her realm in magic, hiding it from the
eyes of us moderns, sick with scepticism, who don't know, and who can no
longer believe in, the beautiful fairytale of yesterday?

AUTHOR'S FOOTNOTES

1. The bibliography concerning the legends of the Sibilline Mountains is copious. This will be seen as we progress through this volume. In the meantime we want to bear in mind various studies containing general bibliographies on the subject: F. DESONAY, *Introduction* to A. DE LA SALE, *Le Paradis de la Reine Sibylle*, Paris 1930, pgs. XI-CXXVII; G. CROCIONI, *Bibliographia delle tradizioni popolari marchigiane*, Firenze, 1953, pp.136-139, nn. 911ss.; L. PAOLUCCI, *La Sibilla appenninica*, Firenze, 1967, pp.71-73.

We also wish to bring attention to the graduate thesis of Romano Cardullo, defended at the Catholic University of the Sacred Heart of Milan in the academic year 1973/74 and conducted under the direction of Professor A. Marinoni. We have had this thesis close at hand up through the first edition of this booklet and we have used it to advantage for various clarifications and bibliographical citations. This is a commendable work which carries a solid contribution to the exploration of our legends, dense with bibliographical and cultural references and valuable for a new Italian translation of the French text of *Paradis de la Reine Sibylle* by A. De La Sale, as well as for various suggestions and indications of new sources.

2. A. FABBI, *Viso e le sue Valli*, Spoleto, 1965, p. 16. He writes, "In the Middle Ages, given the superstition rooted in the mountains and the respect of Christians towards the Sybil, considered as a forseer of the Redeemer on the same level as the prophets, the myth of the grotto continued in literature and in art. On the precipices of the Lago di Pilato and the cliffs of the Mt. Sibilla, Jews and hermits took refuge. Nostalgic for pagan rites, they carried on hedonistic rituals. That occured, according to Fumi (*Eretici e ribelli nell'Umbria e nelle Marche nel sec. XIV*), especially during the exile of Avignon and particularly under the pontificate of John XXII. Among the umbro-marchigian heretics the Paterines were

notable. They supported free love and, to legitimate their passions, they went through sacred rites in honor of the devil, returning thus to the orgiatic rites of paganism."

3. W. PABST, *Venus und die missverstandene Dido,* in *Hamburger Romanistiche Studien,* A. 40, Hamburg, 1955, pp.. 9ss. Cf also F. ALLEVI, *Con Dante la Sibilla ed altri, Milano,* 1965, Pp.. 101- 102.

4. G. B. LALLI, *Tito Vespasiano overo Gerusalemme desolata,* Foligno, 1635, canto II, stanza VII.

5. G. G. TRISSINO, *L'Italia Liberata dai Goti,* in *Tutte le Opere,* edited by S. MAF-FEI, Verona, 1729, book XXIV. Cf. regarding this L. PAOLUCCI, op.cit., pp. 46, 61, and 65. F. ALLEVI, op.cit. pp. 101-103.

6. L. PAOLUCCI, op.cit. pp., 28 and 49.

7. A. DE LA SALE, *Le Paradis de la Reine Sibilla,* edited by F. Desonay, Paris, 1930. This can be read in Italian translation in the anthology of Falzetti, *Il Paradiso della Regina Sibilla,* Norcia, 1963, pp.. 122-68.
A. De La Sale has left us a drawing of two little maps of the grotto and the lake, one colored and the other not, reproduced by Desonay in the cited edition of *Paradis.*

8. L. ALBERTI, *Descrittione di tutta Italia,* Bologna, 1550, p. 248v
Speaking of St. Maria in Gallo (=Montegallo) Alberti writes: "In this vicinity (but known as the Appenines) is the ample, horrid, and frightening cave called the cave of the Sibyl of which in popular report (as a matter of fact wild and crazy tales) there is the entrance by which to reach the Sibyl, who resides in a fine Realm, adorned by grand and magnificent palaces, inhabited by many people, taking amorous pleasures in the aforementioned palaces and gardens with charming damsels. They do this by day, and then at night the men as well as the women become fearful snakes together with the Sibyl, and all those who desire to enter there must first of all take lascivious pleasures with the aforementioned disgusting snakes. And no one is forced to remain here, unless a year has passed. And that it is necessary to remain there forever for those who stay more than a year. And those who were there and then return outside are granted many graces and privileges by the Sibyl, so that they can

happily pass the rest of their days. The people are in the habit of telling this and other similar tales just like I remember hearing told in the house of my father to the women (still being a little boy) to arouse and please".

9. For the geological and naturalistic aspects in general of the Lago di Pilato see: B. TEODORI, *Aspetti idrobiologici del Lago di Pilato nel gruppo dei Monti Sibillini*, in *Natura e Montagna*, June 1967, n.1&2, pp.. 43-48. Teodori was the first to point out the existence of a "branchipod," called *Chirocephalus marchesonii* in homage to Professor V. Marchesoni.

Concerning the Lago di Pilato, one also looks to the studies of G. JAJA, *Excursione nei Sibillini*, Roma, 1905; A CALZECCHI-ONESTI, *I Monti Sibillini*, in *Le Vie d'Italia*, February 1923; C. LIPPI-BONCAMPI, *I Monti Sibilline*, Bologna, 1948; V. MARCHESONI, *Appunti idrobiologici sul lago di Pilato nei Monti Sibillini* (in collaboration with G. MORETTI), in *Bollettino della Societa Eustachiana*, 47, (1954); V. MARCHESONI-G. MORETTI, *Il lago di Pilato nei Monti Sibillini*, in *L'Appenino*, Minutes of the CAI, May-June 1956; P. MARMIL-LI, *Oscillazione di livello dell acqua del lago di Pilato*, ivi, September-October 1956.

10. A. GRAF, *Un Monte di Pilato in Italia*, in *Miti, leggende e superstizione Italia*, Torino, 1925 (I edition 1889), pp.. 339-355. Fundamental study of the legends relative to the lake, above all because the documents of P. Bersuire and Fra Bernardino Bonavoglia di Foligno were published here.

11. During the year 41 AD Baronio wrote: "Sub hac eadem Olympiade ducentesima quarta, anno tertio, Pilatum, olim Judeae Procuratum miseeranda morte interisse Eusebius sribit his verbis; Pontiius Pilate in multas incidens clallmitates, propria se manu interfecit, ut sribunt romani historici. Hoc Eusebius: affirmat idipsum Cassiodorus in Chronico. Viennae autem in Galliis contigisse cum multi referant: Ado, eiusdem civitis Episcopus inhunc modum rem scribit: Pilatus,qui sententiamm damnationis in Christum dixerat et ipse perpetuo exilio Viennae recluditur; tantisque ibi irrogari Caio langoribus coartatus est, ut sua se transverberans manu, multorum malorum compendium mortis celeritate quaesierit. Sunt haec verba Orosii, licet ipse de Vienna nihil. Quod vero recentiorum Graecorum aliqui dicant Pilatum de nece Christi a Maria Magdelena Romae iudicio postulatum, ut commentum refellimus. Ceterum de eius interitu omnes aeque consentiunt, ipsum summ desparatione actum, sibi necem intulisse" *(Annales Ecclesiastici,* Romae, 1593, vol. I, P. 290).

12. The passage of P. Bersuire was quoted by Graf in Italian translation (p.334) and in the original latin (p. 353 n. 19) and also by Paolucci op. cit. p. 53. Fabbi refers to it in the Italian translation op. cit. pp. 12-13. We too for love of completeness transcribe the latin text of P. Bersuire: "Exemplum terribile esse circa Nurciam Italiae civitem audivi pro vero experto narrari a quodam praelato summe inter alios fide digno Dicebat enim inter montes isti civitati proximos esse lacum ab antiquis daemonibus consecratum et ab ipsis sensibiliter inhabitum ad quem nullus hodie tum et ab ipsis sensibiliter inhabitatum ad quem nullus hodie praeter necromanticos potest accedere quin a daemonibus rapiatur. Igitur circa termino lacus facti sunt muri quia custobus servantur ne necromantici pro libris suis consecrandis daemonibusi illuc accedere permittantur. Et ergo istud ibi summe terribile quia civitas illa omni anno unum hominem virum pro tributo infra ambitum murorum ixa lacum ad daemones mittit qui statum visibiliter illum hominem lacerant et consumunt quod (ut aiunt) nisi civitas faceeret patria tempestatibus deperiret. Civitas ergo annuatim sceleratum eligit et pro tributo illus daemonibus mittit. Istud autem quia alicubi non legi, nullatenus crederem, nisi a tanto episcopo firmiter asseri audivissem".

Graf justly observes that in the text of Bersuire there is no allusion to Pilate, although in the 14th century the legend was noted, as pointed out by Fazio degli Uberti (op cit., pp.. 344-345).

13. The Latin passage of Fra Bernardino Bonavoglia is preserved in the Biblioteca Comunale di Foligno under the signature A H II 10; this was communicated by Faloci-Pulignano to Graf, who reproduced it in Italian translation (pp. 345-6) and in the original Latin (pp. 353-4, n.24). Paolucci also refers to it, op.cit., pp. 55-6.

14. Nicolo Peranzoni writes in *De Laudibus Piceni,* Fero, 1795, p. 117: "Duo ibi circuli super lapides incisi iuxta lacus marginem quibusdam characteribus mostrantur, quos ad artem magicam consequendam necessarios aiunt eorumque, alterum Virgilium mantuanum poetam, alterum vero Ciccum Auscuanum mathematicum effinxisse praedicant." Cf also L. PAOLUCCI, op. cit.pp. 18 and 59.

15. G. CROCIONI, *La gente marchigiana nelle sue tradizioni,* Milano, 1951, p. 146.

16. A. FABBI op.cit. p. 15, n. 11.

17. P. PIRRI, *L'Archivo di Castello di Ussita,* Isola del Liri, 1932, pp. 50-1; cf. Also A. FABBI., op. cit. p. 246 and F. ALLEVI, op. cit. pp. 46-7 and 118.

18. A. FABBI, op.cit., p. 246, n. 167. Fabbi writes: "Magic must have been common in the 14th century from what one can deduce from the Reformation of Guaita of 7-6-1433, in which the recurring popular terms of astrology and astrologers are always in use: Cum certi incantatores vestiti in form fratrum vadant per dictum vallem Uxitae incantando et extorlocando, dicendo velle invenire thesaurum sub terram iacentem per artem ymagicam et diabolicam quod displicet Deo et eius sanctis, et posset in dicta Guaita Uxitae magnum scandalum edt errorem generare, deliberaverunt quod usquequo vineae non fuerint vindemmiatae nullus de dicta valle Uxitae debeaat se intromictere in cavando aliquod thesaurum(...) Et quod nullus de dicta Uxitae possit nec debeat aliquem strollacum seu strollicum retinere."

19. Cf. D. FALZETTI, *I Monti Sibillini e i paesi circostanti,* in *Il Paradiso della Regina Sibilla, cit.,* p.197.

20. A. VITTORI, *Montemonaco nel regno della Sibilla Appennina,* Firenze, 1938, p.130; cf. also F. ALLEVI, op.cit., pp. 111-112.

21. P. TOSCHI, *Prefazione* to *La Sibilla Appenninica* by PAOLUCCI, cit., pp. IX- X.

22. L. PAOLUCCI, op.cit., pp. 65-66.

23. C. PICCOLPASSO, *Le piante e i ritratti delle citta e terre dell'Umbria sottoposte al governo di Perugia,* edited by G. CECCHINI, Istituto nazionale di Archeologia e Storia dell'arte, Roma; cf. also D. FALZETTI, op.cit., pp. 217-19; F. ALLEVI, op.cit., p.45, n.3.

23.b. *L'Editto generale del S. Offizio* was published in Ancona by N. Baluffi in 1829. We quote the long passage of the examination of conscience of St. Giacomo della Marca, published by G. FABIANI, *Ascoli nel Cinquecento,* Ascoli Piceno, 1971, p.400, which deals with the Notarial Archive of that city, and referred to also by U. PICCIAFUOCO, *S. Giacomo della Marca,* Montepradone, 1976, pp.35-36, n.32: "*...If you took or applied the red hot iron to demonstrate some truth or another thing. If you believe in charms, fates, and dreams. If you believe that by encountering certain spirits, you will follow them for good or* *evil. If you believe that someone born in a certain hour will be cursed or blessed. If you believe that the planets and constellations compel man to do evil. If you believe in soothsayers and enchantresses. If you have believed that women or human bodies go around at night and become witches, cats, or wolves and drink the blood of babies and similar practices. If you uses herbs against demons. If you have a ring or knot or symbol on cord to wear around the neck or back. If you have cast spells or had spells cast against Christians of various infirmities of the teeth or flesh...or head. If you have cast spells to the moon or the sun or the stars. If you have cast spells to discover theft or to have it done. If you have counseled someone to cast similar spells. If you have used spells or cast spells to do evil and used holy water or sacred things. If you have worshiped herbs or elder flower or other creatures in similar spells or deeds. If you have foretold with cards or with olive palms... or opening books or otherwise. If you have had said or said masses or other prayers against someone and such then died or bad things then happened to such a person . If you have owned books of assorted spells and similar things and if you do not burn them nobody can absolve you."*

24. A.VITTORI, op.cit.,pp.129-130.

25. A.FABBI, op.cit.,p.246, n.167. The verses are passages of a poem in the native dialect: *Lu fiju de Jampa*.

26. G.B. MILIANI, *I monti della Sibilla*, Roma, 1892, pp. 5ss. In this booklet of 37 pages one reads various and delightful legends of the Sibilline region.

27. A. GRAF,op. cit. p. 355. Graf quotes word for word the lecture of Professor Vincenzo Ghinassi of the school of Spoleto.

28. G. CROCIONI,   *La gente marchigiana nelle sue tradizioni,* cit., p. 141.

29. The first edition of *Guerin Meschino* is that published in Padua in 1473, but subsequent editions, often incorrect, multiplied up into our century. Fairly widespread is the one published by the editor Bietti, Milano, 1904, which notwithstanding that it is presented as the "most complete edition," inspires very little confidence for a rigorous philological study; nonetheless it is sufficient for a complete recall of the facts (for our discussion see Book V, pp. 168-83).

120

One might also enjoy reading *Guerin Meschino* in the edition "compiled for the readers of the 20th century," brought to light by Vanzetti, Milano, 1923 but as with every abridgement, it is more or less unreliable.

We too give a loose version here of the legend of Meschino, but not definitive as to the plot and the facts.

30. F. HEMMERLIN, *De nobilitate et rusticate dialogus,* Basilea, 1497, p. XCII. Desonay points out that the discussion of Hemmerlin was composed in the years 1444-1450. (*Introduction, cit., pp. CXII-CXIV*).

31. A. OERTEL, *Theatrum orbis terrarum,* Antuerpia, 1572, p.67. The Latin passage is also quoted by Paolucci, op.cit.,pp.62-63.

32. L. PULCI, *Lettere a Lorenzo il Magnifico e ad altri,* Lucca, 1868, p.42. Paolucci, op.cit., p.57, quotes this passage of the letter, addressed to "Magnificent and generous Laurentio Petri de Medici": "The bearer is a horseman from Bologna. Note that he is the one who carried that letter from Messer Giovanni Bentivogli the Wednesday of the devils. By him you have the truffles that Maestro Bastiano left me which I send to you on his account. And meanwhile I will go to Norcia and conveyed by the Sibyl I will send you some more of them so that you will have them fresher and not all at one time". On the visit of Pulci to the Sibilline places, cf. in particular G. VOLPE, in *Giornale Storico della Letteratura Italiana,* XXII (1893).

33. G. BONOMO, *Uno stregone trentino e un viaggio al Monte della Sibilla,* in *Caccia alle streghe,* Palermo, 1954, pp. 74-78. Cf. also F. ALLEVI, op. cit., p. 31.

34. Desonay writes in the cited *Introduction,* p. XXXII, n. 1: "Nous supposerons donc que le chatelain facetieux (il s'etait mis a rire quand le visiteur lui avait exprime son desir de pousser jusq'au mont de Venus) aura fait prendre a son hote des vessies pour...une caverne, quelques trous proches dans le roc appennin pour la grotte misterieuse qu'Arnolf ne devait point voir. Ainsi tout s'esplique: et la deception du pelerin, et linvraisemblance de la narration".

Cf. Also A. REUMONT, *Viaggio in Italia nel 1497 del cav. Arnolfo di Harff di Colonia sul Reno,* text, introduction and notes, in *Archivio Veneto,* IX (1876), pp. 124-146, 393-407; then in *Saggi di Storia e letterature,* Firenze, 1880.

Here is the text of Arnolfo di Harff as it is in the cited study by Reumont: "Near Norde (Norcia) is situated the Mountain of Venus, on which slope there is a castle guarded by a chatelaine of the Pope We made contact with him and told him in latin that it was our intention to climb Mt. Venus of which many stories are told in our country. The lord of the castle laughed (...). The next morning we rode together towards the mountain, which is carved with many grottos and tunnels (...) We entered in the named grotto without, however, seeing anything. On the mountain there is a little lake next to which is a little chapel with a little altar. At which, according to the lord of the castle, in the time of necromancy, they performed exorcisms during which the water of the lake rose up in the form of a cloud falling back to earth with a crash like thunder and flooding all the country, so that one couldn't harvest. The people complained to the lord of the castle, who then erected a gallows between the chapel and the lake with prohibitions of any acts of necromancy. Our host said he didn't know anything else about that place."

35. L. ALBERTI, op. cit. pp. 248v.-249r. Cf. F. ALLEVI, op.cit., p.122.

36. Cf. D. FALZETTI, *Gli scavi sul Monte Sibilla*, in *Il Paradiso della Regina Sibilla*, cit., pp. 36ss, which records various dates from the 16th century, carved in the cave and collected during the excavations of 1953; cf. A. GRAF, op. cit., p. 347.

37. For these scientific surveys cf. the *Introduzione* by V. RICCI to LANDI VITTORI's book, *Appennino Centrale*, CAI-TCI, Milano, 1955, and F. RODOLICO, *L'esplorazione naturalistica dell'Appennino*, Firenze, 1963.

38. FAZIO DEGLI UBERTI, *Il Dittamondo e le Rime*, edited by G. CORSI, Bari, Laterza, 1952, vol.1, p.186.

39. G. CROCIONI, *La gente marchigiana nelle sue tradizioni*, cit.,p.150; cf.also G. ORCIANI, *Scariotto patria di Giuda nella Marca anconitana*, Montecarotto, 1914.

40. Graf also quotes these words of commentary on the verses of Fazio, credited to CAPELLO: " The Mountain of Pilate they say is above Norcia, and there is a place of devils, to which go those who want to understand the magical arts" (A. GRAF, op.cit., p.345).

41. L. PULCI, *Il Morgante*, edited by G. FATINI, Torino, UTET, 1968, vol. II. It is known that *Il Morgante* came out in its first edition in 1478 with 23 cantos and then in a second edition in 1483 with 28 cantos. Cf. also F. ALLEVI, op.cit., p.117; L. PAOLUCCI, op.cit., pp.57-58.

42. The *Farsa dello Ymagico* was published by F. TORRACA in *Studi di letteratura napoletana*, Livorno, 1884, pp.283-284. Cf. also F. ALLEVI, op.cit., pp.122-123, L. PAOLUCCI, op.cit., p.56.

43. E.S. PICCOLOMINI, *Epistolario*, Lib. I, Ep. 46, in *Opera*, Basilea, 1571. PAOLUCCI, in op.cit., pp.54-55, quotes the letter in an Italian translation, which appeared in the Sunday supplement of *Il progresso italo-americano* (New York) on April 10, 1932.

44. F. BIONDO, *De Roma instaurata* (...) *De Italia illustrata, Italy Illuminated Jeffrey A White trans.* I Tatti Renaissance Library, Harvard University Press, 2005
Torino, 1527, p. 84v. Cf. L. PAOLUCCI, op. cit., p.54.

45. Cf. F. ALLEVI, op. cit., p. 105.

46. B. SPAGNOLI, *Nicolaus tolentinus*, book. I and book. II in *Opera*, Paris, 1913; also in *De sacris diebus*,, wherein Mantovano makes a fleeting reference to the Norcian Sibyl. Cf. also the cited text of R. CORDELLA.

47. F. PANFILO, *Picenum, hoc est de agro Piceni quae Anconitana vulgo Marchia nominatur nobiltate et laudibus opus,* in G. COLUCCI, *Antichita Picene*, Fermo, 1786, volume XVI, Book III, p. CLIII.
Panfilo was a scribe at the council of Trent. Cf. also A. CANALETTI GAUDENTI, *Francesco Panfilo umanista sanseverinate del Cinquecento e il suo poema Picenum,* in *Studia Picena*, XV (1940); F. ALLEVI, op. cit., pp. 90-91.

48. N. PERANZONI, *De laudibus Piceni, sive Marchiae anconitanae libellus,* in G. COLUCCI, *Antichita Picene,* Fermo, 1795, volume XXV, pp. 117-18. The passage is also referred to by PAOLUCCI, op. cit., pp. 58-6.

49. L. ALBERTI, op. cit., p. 248v.

50. We are helped by TEODORI (article cited, pp. 45-6) who after surveying the karstic- glacial action of the Lago di Pilato, thus explains the cause of the "strange oscillation of the lake's level".

"One might be led to believe that the maximum flooding of the two lake basins happens in winter; on the contrary the maximum flooding coincides on average with the beginning of summer, when the thawing of the snows is strong, or in autumn when there is abundant precipitation. In winter the lake, as was observed in the years 1953-56, is more or less empty; one deduces from the presence of concentric circles subsiding from the frozen surface of the lake basins. The phenomena can be explained in this way; the first signs of cold weather find the surface of the lake (m1940) open wide to the north and protected on all other sides, with the maximum filling; the temperature which plunges notably below zero centigrade, determines the freezing of it. The layers of ice function as covers of the basins. Nevertheless, the waters under the ice flow out through the karstic paths in the deepest, coldest part of the lake... In this way it creates a layer of air between the upper ice and the open surface of the water. The icy layer quickly breaks into concentric circles when weighed down by snowy precipitation, since is not supported below, it falls into the water or sinks onto the shore. At this point the surface of the lake, returned into contact with the bite of the cold winds, freezes and the process begins again.

It is believed however that the lake basins are never totally without water, because the layers of ice, which continue to thicken, eventually come to lean bit by bit on the defined shoreline and can support the weight of the thick blanket of snow (which can reach 10 meters). On the other hand the melting at the base of the ice assures the replenishment of the lake, compensating for the continual karstic outflow." On this topic cf. also P. MARMILLI, *Oscillazioni di livello delle acque del lago di Pilato*, cit., and E. BEVILAQUA , *Marche,* UTET, Torino, 1961, p.81.

51. L. ARIOSTO, *Orlando Furioso*, edited by N. ZINGARELLI, Milano, Hoepli, 1959. Cf. also L. PAOLUCCI, op.cit., p.66. Translation by Guido Waldman, Oxford World Classics, Oxford University Press, New York 1974.

52. G.G. TRISSINO, *L'Italia liberata dai Goti*, in *Tutte le Opere*, edited by S. MAFFEI, Verona, 1729. Cf. also F. ALLEVI, op.cit., pp.102-104; L. PAOLUCCI, op.cit., pp. 61-62.

124

53. F. BERNI, *Rime*, edited by G. BARBERI-SQUAROTTI, Torino, Einaudi, 1969, p.22. The editor is not convincing when he writes in a footnote that "The Sibyl was in no way from Norcia, but here Berni perhaps alludes to the caverns, numerous in the mountains of Umbria, and from that the image of the Sibyl came to him." In reality our Sibyl is often called by the writers "nursina", that is, of Norcia. Cf. also F. TORRACA, *Nuove rassegne*, Livorno, 1894, p.179; L. PAOLUCCI, op.cit., p. 67.

54. P. ARETINO, *Scritti Scelti*, edited by G.G. FERRERO, Torino, UTET, 1970, p. 364. One knows that the *Ragionamento* together with the *Dialogo* make up the work titled *Sei giornate*.

55. B. CELLINI, *La Vita*, edited by E. CARRARA and G.G. FERRERO, Torino, UTET, 1968, pp.200-205. The episode goes back to 1532.

56. A.F. DONI, *Inferni*, Venezia, 1553. Cf. regarding this F. TORRACA, *Nuove Rassegne*, cit., p.179.

57. A.F. DONI, *I Marmi*, edited by E. CHIORBOLI, Bari, Laterza, 1928, p. 219.

58. A. OERTEL, *Theatrum orbis terrarum*, Antuerpia, 1572, p. 67. The passage about the Sibilline legends is also quoted by PAOLUCCI, op.cit., pp. 62-63.

59. G.A. MAGINI, *Descrittione universale della terra*, Padova, 1621, p.90. Paolucci also refers to this passage, op.cit., p. 63.

60. P. MERULA, *Cosmographia Generalis*, Amsterdam, 1621, p. 579. The passage by Merula was pointed out by Graf, who reprinted it in op.cit., p. 354, n. 29, and it was then also reprinted by PAOLUCCI, op.cit., p.64.

61. L. BEYERLINK, *Magnum theatrum vitae humanae*, Lione, 1678, vol.VII, p. 243. He writes, "De loco Sibyllarum varie fabulantur veteres. Sententia communior in Piceno eas habitasse circa Montem Appenninum".

62. T. D'ARAGONA, *Il Meschino and il Guerino*, Venezia, 1560. The poem is in

"eighth rhyme." Cf. the argument of P. RAJNA, *Ricerche intorno ai Reali di Francia,* Bologna, 1872; G. AMADIO, *La Sibilla Appenina nel poema di Tullia D'Aragona,* in *Vita Picena,* August 22, 1942.

63. G.B.LALLI, *Tito Vespasiano overo Gerusalemme desolata,* Foligno, 1635. Cf. In this regard F. TORRACA, *Nuova rassegne,* ci. Pp. 180-2; L. PAOLUCCI, op. cit., pp. 64-5; F. ALLEVI pp. 70, 105, n. 17, 128; A. FABBI, op. cit., p. 15, n. 11, which informs us that Lalli, in his other poem *Moschiede* describes the miserable end of Alcabizio at the Lago di Pilato.

64. F. ALLEVI, op. cit., pp. 128-30.

65. G. PARINI, *Il Giorno, (Il Mattino,* vv. 1066-1073), edited by G. M. ZURADELLI, Milano, UTET, 1968. pp. 234-35.

66. W. GOETHE, *Faust,* edited by G. MANACORDA, Milano, 1949, p.364. Cf. also in this regard F. ALLEVI, op. cit., p. 119

67. A. SARTORIO, *La Sibilla,* Milano, 1922. Cf. in this regard G. CROCIONI, *La gente marchigiana nelle sue tradizioni,* cit., pp. 445-46, and *Bibliografia delle tradizioni popolari marchigiane,* cit., p. 138, n. 935; L. PAOLUCCI, op. cit., p. 65.

68. D. TUMIATI, *Guerin Meschino, Leggenda drammatica in tre atti,* Milano, 1912. Here one can also remember that in 1920 *Guerin Meschino* was staged by the musician Adriano Linaldi (Alastor) with libretto by Cavicchioli (cf. G. AMADIO, *Scave sul Monte Sibilla,* in *Toponomastica marchigiana,* Ascoli, 1954, p. 140-44).

69. F. TOMBARI, *Tutta Frusaglia,* Milano, Mondadori, 1968, cantafavola XI (first edition, 1927).

70. G. TITTA ROSA, *Fra il Lago e il Monte della Sibilla,* in *Le vie d'Italia,* May 1941, pp. 529-537.

71. G. PIOVENE, *Viaggio in Italia,* Mondadori, 1971, p. 410.

126

72. T. COLSALVATICO, *Lo spirito di una terra*, in *Le Marche* (special number of the *Rivista di Ancona*), 1961, pp. 14 and 23-6.

73. Cf. N. MANCINI, *La leggenda del Guerin Meschino e della Sibilla picena in due poemetti dialettali*, in *Il Messaggero*, edited for Le Marche, June 28, 1942; cf. Also G. CRO-CIONI, *Bibliografia delle tradizioni popolari marchigiane*, cit., p. 138, n. 933.

74. F. JESI, *Sui passi di Guerin Meschino*, in *Storia illustrata*, May 1964, pp. 688-700, with photographs by E. BUSULINI.

75. Cf. R. WAGNER, *Tannhäuser*, introduction and editorial commentary by G. MAN-ACORDA, Firenze, 1938. Cf. in this regard F. DESONAY, *Il paradiso della Regina Sibilla*, in A. VITTORI *Montemonaco*, etc. cit., p. 173.

76. Cf. P. RAJNA, *Nei paraggi della Sibilla di Norcia*, in *Studi dedicati a F. Torraca, nel XXXVI anniverssario dell sua laurea*, Napoli, 1912, pp. 333-53; A. REUMNOT, *Del Monte di Venere, ossia Labirinto d'amore*, in *Archivo Storico Italiano*, XIII (1871), pp. 376ss., then in *Saggi di Storia e Letteratura*, Firenze, 1880. Pp. 378ss.
Of D. PARIS see in particular: *Le Paradis de la Reine Sibylle*, in *Revue de Paris*, 15 December 1897, reprinted in *Legendes du moyen age*, Paris, 1903, pp. 65ss., where one reads interesting pages about *Paradis* of A. DE LA SALE and Tannhäuser.

77. A. GRAF. *Un Monte di Pilato in Italia*, Torino, 1889, then in *Miti, leggende, e superstizioni del Medioevo*, Torino, 1925, pp. 339-53.

78. F. TORRACA, *Nuove rassegne*, Livorno, 1894, pp. 179-81; see also *Studi di letteratura napoletana*, Livorno, 1884, pp. 283-4 and p. 432.

79. F. NERI, *Le leggende italiane della Sibilla*, in *Studi Medioevali*, IV (1912-13), pp. 213-30; then in *Ricerche di storia letteraturia*, (Fabrilia), Torino, 1930.

80. W. SÖDERHJELM, A. *De La Sale et la legende de Tannhäuser*, in *Memoirs* of the *Societe neo-philologique a Helsingers*, II (1897), pp. 111-67.

81. H. DÜBI, *Frau Veren und der Tannhäuser,* in *Zeitschrift der Vereins fur umlaut Volkskunde,* XVII (1907). Pp. 249ss.

82. F. DESONAY, *Introduction* to *Le paradis de la Reine Sibylle* of A. De La Sale, Paris, 1930. There are various publications by Desonay on the subject: *A. De La Sale avventureux et pedagogue,* Liege Paris, 1940; *Le fonti italiane della leggende del Tannhäuser,* in *Il paradiso dell Regina Sibilla* of FALZETTI, Norcia, 1963; *Il paradiso della Regina Sibilla,* in A. VITTORI, op.cit., pp. 173-833; etc.

83. G. SPERANZA, Il Piceno, *Ascoli P.,* 1900.

84. G. CROCIONI, *La gente marchigiana nelle sue tradizioni,* Milan, 1951; *Bibliografia delle tradizioni popolari marchigiane,* Firenze, 1953.

85. A. VITTORI, *Montemonaco-Nel regno della Sibilla apennina,* Firenze, 1938. In the *Appendice* he quotes studies by Desonay, Amadio, and Monti Guarnieri on the Sibyl.

86. G. AMADIO, *Toponomastica marchigiana,* Ascoli P., 1953, vol. II; La Sibilla, in A. VITTORI, op. cit., pp. 185-91.

87. L. PAOLUCCI, *La Sibilla Appenninica,* Firenze, 1967, con *Prefazione* di P. TOSCHI (pp. III-XVI). Fundamental study for in depth discussions and abundant documentation.

88. D. FALZETTI, *Il Paradiso della Regina Sibilla,* Norcia, 1963.

89. A. FABBI, *Leggende dei Sibillini,* in *Visso e le sue Valli,* Spoleto, 1965, pp. 12-17, and *passim.*

90. F. ALLEVI, *Con Dante la Sibilla e altri,* Milano, 1965; cf. also *Il Balcone della Sibilla,* Milano, 1960.

91. W. PABST, *Venus und die missverstandene Dido,* in *Hamburger Romantische Studien,* A. 40, Hamburg, 1955, pp. 9ss.

92. M. WIS, *Ursprünge der deutschen Tannhäuser Legende*, in *Neuphilologische Miteilungen (Helsinki), I LXI (1960*.

93. For a quite detailed bibliographical review we refer you to the oft cited *Introduction* of Desonay, preface to the *Paradis* of A. De La Sale, pp. LXXXIIIss,; to G. CROCIONI, *Bibliografia delle tradizioni popolari marchigiane,* cit., pp. 136-39, nn. 911-948; to L. PAOLUCCI, op., cit., *Bibliografia, pp. 71-3*; and to the dense notes of the cited study by F. ALLEVI, *Con Dante la Sibilla e altri.* Here for love of completeness, we want to indicate those studies which we have not had the opportunity to mention in other parts of this volume: R. RENIER, *La discesa d'Ugo d'Alvernia all'Inferno,* Bologna, 1883 (here one reads a bibliography of *Guerin Meschino*); G. GAVASSI, *Montemonaco e la leggenda della Sibilla,* in *Picenum*, I (1910), 366-367; R. RENIER, *Guerin Meschino*, in *Fanfulla della Domenica,* XXXIV (1912), n. 23; C. CALZONI, *Passeggiate umbre: Norcia e la grotta della Sibilla,* in *La Tribuna,* August 22, 1922; A. DEL MOSCIO, *Visioni e leggende di Monti-Sulla cima del Monte Vettore,* in *Rassegna Marchigiana per le arti figurative, le bellezze naturali e la musica,* December 1922; Idem, *Nel regno della Sibilla,* in *Il Tempo, September 21, 1925;* D. FALZETTI, *La grotta dell Sibilla di Norcia e il lago di Pilato,* in *Il Messaggero,* October 16, 1925; I. FENIZI, *L'antica regina del Tenna-Faleria Picena,* in *Rassegna marchigiana,* cit. October 1925; B. FATTORI, *All ricerca di Pilato,* ivi, December 1925; G. BELLONCI, *Sul Monti di Sibilla in cerca di Tannhäuser,* in *Giornale d'Italia,* June 22, 1926; B. FATTORI, *Da Pretara a S. Maria dell'Ambro,* in *Rassega marchigiana,* cit., January 1927; V. FRENGUELLI, *Un mistero inviolato: la grotta della Sibilla,* ivi, August 14, 1927; A. F. GUIDI, *Dove le Sibille italiche non sono morte,* in *Il lavoro d'Italia,* September 28, 1928; A. MAURIZI, *Casteluccio e i Monti Sibillini,* l'Aquila, 1931; L. FREUND, *Studien zur Belgeschicht der Sibillen,* Hamburg, 1932; G. OSELLA, *Il Guerin Meschino,* Torino, 1932 (with a bibliography for *Guerino,* pp.11-12, and for the Sibyl, pp.45-50, 113-125); A. MAURIZI, *Alpinismo e la letteratura sul Vettore,* l'Aquila, 1934; T. FABIANI, *Il Paradiso della Regina Sibilla,* in *Toga praetexta* (Ascoli Piceno), I (1934), issues 3-4, pp.76-79; C. MARIOTTI, *Intorno alla leggenda della Sibilla,* in *Nostre regioni,* (Ascoli Piceno), II (1946); P. PICCOLOMINI, *Pretare paese delle fate,* ivi, III (1947); L. NADA, *La Sibilla nel poema di A. Sertorio,* in *Giornale d'Italia,* edition for Le Marche, October 5, 1941; G. CAPRIN, *Il Paradiso della Sibilla,* in *Il Resto del Carlino,* August 30, 1957; C. UGOLINO, *L'infernaccio,* in *Voce del Santuario Madonna dell'Ambro,* X (1964), n.26; Idem, *La leggenda del lago di Pilato,* ivi, XV (1969), n.35; Idem, *La leggenda della*

Sibilla, ivi XV (1969), n.36; G. SANTARELLI, *La sinistra fama del lago di Pilato*, ivi, XX (1974), June, pp.10-11; Idem, *La grotta fatata della Sibilla*, ivi, XX (1974) December, pp.10-11; C. UGOLINI, *Le leggende dei Monti Sibillini*, ivi, XX (1974), December, pp.14-15; G. LISOTTI, *Le leggende dei Monti Sibillini*, in *Il Marchigiano*, December 12 1974, pp. 23-24; CIZETA, *Paesaggi marchigiani- La grotta della Sibilla*, in *Notizie da Palazzo Albani*, 1975, n.1, pp.49-54; etc., etc.

94. For more exhaustive information in these regards cf., aside from the cited *Introduction* by DESONAY, the study recalled above by M. WIS, which offers a quite diligent index of the various hypotheses under discussion. In the following we cite, all together, the authors named in these pages and not cited elsewhere: E. SCHMIDT, *Charakteristiken*, Berlin, 1912; E. ELSTER, *Tannhäuser in Geschichte Sage und Dichtung*, Ein Vortrag gehalten October 7,1907, Bromberg 1908; K. REUSCHEL, *Die Tannhäusersage, Antrittsvorlesung gehaten in der Technischen Koch-schule zu Dresden am 27 okt.1903, Neue Jahrbücher für das Klassische Altertum, Geschichte und deutsche Literatur*, VII (1904), p.653; R.M. MEYER, *Tannhäuser und die Tannhäusersage*, in *Zeitschrift des Vereins fur Volkskunde*, XXI (1911), pp.1-31; F. KLUGE, *Bunte Blätter-Kulturgeschichtliche Vorträge und Aufsätse*, Freiburg (Baden), 1908; F. PFAFF, *Die Tannhäusersage, Verhandlungen der 49 Versammlung deutschen Philologen und Schulmänner*, 1907, Leipzig, 1908, pp.104ss.; J. GRIMM, *Deutsche Mithologie*, Berlin,1876; PH.S. BARTO, *Studies in the Tannhäuserlegende*, in *Journal of English and Germanic Philology*, IX (1910), n.3, pp. 293-320; *The German Venusberg*, ivi, XII (1913), n.2.

95. F. ALLEVI, op. cit., pp. 30-31.

96. M. WIS, op cit., pp. 50ss.

97. Cf. F. NERI, op. cit., p. 10; F. DESONAY, *Introduction*, cit., p. XCVI, n. 3; F. ALLEVI, op cit., p. 110; L. PAOLUCCI, op. cit., p.24 and passim.

98. This tradition of a Sibyl jealous of the divine maternity of Mary is diametrically opposed to another which sees instead the ancient prophetess exalted by the supreme privilege of the Madonna. Thus, for example, one reads in an 18th century repertory addressed to preachers, "We don't think, says Pietro Canisio, that it happened without a certain

Providence of God, that a Sibyl, before the word of God took human form, preached to the gentiles her Incarnation, and rejoiced over the Virgin Mary, again before she was happily born, that she was to be given to conceive the King of Heaven and Earth with these words: rejoice oh fortunate maiden, because he who has created the heaven and earth has given to you an infinite and eternal joy, and will be your prisoner, because he will be locked up in your belly, and he will help you in every one of your cares with unfailing support and immortal light–Pietro Canisio, in book 3 of Maria Vergine, chapter 3" (Cf. G. B. MATTIOLI, *Selva historiale di diversi esempi,,* Venezia, 1691, part I, p. 379).

99. Cf. in this regard, L. PAOLUCCI, op. cit., pp. 5-6.

100. Speranza is of the opinion that the Appenine Sibyl is connected with the Cumaen Sibyl, transported to our mountains perhaps by the Umbrians, who could have participated in the famous war of Cuma in 472 B.C. as allies of the Etruscans. Nevertheless Speranza doesn't ignore the medieval components in the evolution of the myth of our Sibyl. He writes: "Thus of their spread [of the Pelasgi] in these places there is the evidence of the group of the Sibilline Mts. In our opinion they were called this by the oracles, who according to tradition dedicated themselves to the Sibyl, confused with the Cumaen Sibyl. Mixed into the prophetic recesses of these mountains, however, is a certain amount of medieval fantasy."

101. Rajna writes on the wings of enthusiasm, "The seat and temple of the gods were in a remote age the summits of mountains: and I have only to pronounce the names of Olympia of Asia and Olympia of Thessaly, of the one and the other Ida, of Dodoneo Tmaro, of Parnassus, of Pindus, because the memories fill the mind of anyone. On the other hand the caves were sacred, sacred because mysterious and because they seemed to be entrances to otherworldly kingdoms [...] The grotto of the Sibyl has the singular quality of being situated virtually at the summit, and that summit, already respectable for its altitude of more than 2000 meters, has the even more singular characteristic of appearing to wear a crown, with its symbolic meaning of the highest degree through all the history of humanity. And one can also see on the band of rock a priestly fillet, symbol of holiness. One says after everything, even if it is rash conjecture, that the cave of the Sibyl was a cult site well before Rome a extended its dominion over this region." (*Nei paraggi della Sibilla di Norcia,* cit., pp.252ss.).

For DESONAY, cf. the cited *Introduction,* p. X; he quotes Rajna, observing that De La Sale speaks of "sieges entaillez tout entours," which, as Rajna supposes, at one time came to light, "but one could believe them to be the work of shepherds who pasture the sheep up there."

102. Desonay writes regarding this: "The myth of the Sibyl one can see rising out of the pagan cult of Cibele, the "Magna Mater" of the Romans, goddess of the mountains, lakes, springs, honored erotically in the ritual grotto, under the symbolic crown [...]. It is noted that the cult of Cibele, introduced from Phrygia in 204 BC, had by the imperial age become wide-spread in the mountain regions of the Appenines and particularly at the foot of the Sibilline Mts. (at Falerone, for example). Cibele is a crowned goddess: as we know the grotto of the Sibilla opens up below the crown of the mountains. Cibele is honored as the goddess of water, of lakes, of springs: we know that a lake, called the lake 'of the queen Sibyl" lies on the mountain, not far from the grotto; on the other side the Aso, a rapid torrent, gushes at the feet of the Sibilla, and two medicinal springs (another particularity of the cult of Cibele) quench the thirst of shepherds and sheep on the rocky peaks. Antoine De La Sale speaks of the seats "entaillez tout entour": it is likely that by excavating one can find the seats all around there." PAOLUC-CI (op. cit., pp. 8-15), opposes the thesis of Desonay, finding the weak point of the studious Belgian in the impossible demonstration of the transformation from the goddess Cibele to the sorceress Sibyl: the one existed with no connection to the other.

103. Cf. L. ALLEVI, *I Monti Sibillini e l'eredita di Cibele* in *Piceno religioso nell'antichita*, Ascoli P., 1940, p. 163. PAOLUCCI (op. cit., p. 13) does not share the thesis of the assibilation that would determine the passage from the word "Cibele" to the word "Sibilla," maintained by L. ALLEVI. He writes: "We respond in brief to Allevi that the "C" in "Cibele" is hard in Latin like the "e" in Greek and that the aforesaid phenomena can never be verified."

FEBO ALLEVI, however, associating himself with the scholar of the same last name, writes: "The transformation of the word "Cibele" into "Sibilla" could also be verified by the phonetic fact of the assibilation of the sound "Cy" to "Si", since in the popular pronunciation beginning in the 3rd century A.D. and throughout the high medieval age, the sound of "c" in front of "a,i,o,y" was palatized, and also by the attenuation of the hard sound of the "k" at the beginning of the Greek "Kibele", conserved in the Latin" (op.cit. p.91).

Here it is not out of place to mention that some scholars, like G.CASTELLI (*La vita e le opere di Cecco d'Ascoli*, Bologna, 1892, p.79) and E. RICCI (*Marche*, Torino, 1929, p.73), are of the hypothesis that the name of our Sibyl and of the homonymous mountain of Piceno are linked to the same root from which is derived the name of "Sabini" or "Sabelli", "from which," observes L.ALLEVI (op.cit., p.91, n.4) "one goes to think of one of those old 'Sabines' or 'Sabelles' in Horace's memoirs (Serm. I, IX, v.29-30), who in Rome exercised the art of divination." RICCI writes literally: "Perhaps they were Sabellis or Sabines, it is rather more certain of that prophetess or Sibyl who gave the name, their name- "Sabellini"- to the chain, which some also call Monti Ascolani" (p.73).

It is to be noted, moreover, that in one of the well-informed accounts of the noted Ptolemaic maps from the middle of the 15th century our mountain is shown as "Sibile", "Sibilie", and "Cibilie" (Cod. Vat. lat.5693 in the year 1469) Cf. in this regard F.ALLEVI, op.cit.,p.91, n.4.

However, in the noted *Galleria delle Carte Geographiche del Vaticano*, in the section *Camerino e il suo territorio* (1580), our mountain is clearly individuated, with a large indication of the cave, under which one reads: *Grotta della Sibilla*.

104. AMADIO writes: "The Appennine Sibyl is for me of Etruscan origin, and therefore more ancient than the one Speranza supposes, and if linked to a Cuma, she is linked to the Cuma of Asia Minor (south of Caico, not far from Focea), precisely where the Etruscans came from." (G.AMADIO, *La Sibilla*, in A.VITTORI, op.cit.,pp.185-186). A little further he adds: "From the name of Cibele, of Kupera, is derived the city name of Cupra, like the Dante-esque Sibilia, developed around a primitive abode" (p.189).

105. L. PAOLUCCI, op.cit., pp.9-10 and p.24.

106. In reconstructing this quick history of the excavation of the grotto of the Sibyl we are aided above all by P. RAJNA, *Nei paraggi della Sibilla di Norcia*, cit., pp. 240ss.; F. DESONAY, *Introduction,* cit., pp. XXXII and LII-LX; *Il Paradiso della Regina Sibilla*, in A. VITTORI, op.cit., pp. 173-83; D. FALZETTI, *Gli scavi nella grotta del Monte Sibilla*, Roma, 1954; G. AMADIO, *Scavi sul Monte Sibilla*, in *Toponomastica marchigiana*, Ascoli P., 1954, vol. III, pp. 140-149, n. 989; F. ALLEVI, op. cit., p. 30, n.14.

107. G.B. MILIANI, op.cit. p.22.

108. DESONAY (*Introduction*, cit., pp. LVIII-LIX) observes bitterly, "C'est la qu'est encastree-malheursemente-la plaque commemorative du Club Alpin d'Ascoli, la qu'une moltitude d'amis de la Sibylle ont cru d'avoir graver dans le roc noms e dates." And fur-

ther along (p. LX, n. 1) he deplores the conventioneers who chose to place this marble slab of considerable dimensions right on an important face of the rock, and quotes approvingly the ironic inscription drafted by Ugo Battaglia on August 13, 1920, on the occasion of Falzetti's first expedition: "Later we arrived up there without a stone, on foot from Norcia, to try to break into the grotto."

109. M. MONTI GUARNIERI, *Per gli scavi nella grotta del Monte Sibilla*, Fermo, 1921; reprinted in A. VITTORI, op. cit., pp. 169-72, and in G. AMADIO, *Scavi sul Monte Sibilla*, in *Toponomastica marchigiane,* cit., pp. 140-142.

110. Cf. G. BELLONCI, in *Il giornale d'Italia,* August 22, 1926.

111. D. FALZETTI, op.cit., p.47.

112. F. DESONAY, *Il Paradiso della Regina Sibilla,* in A. VITTORI, op.cit., pp. 175-76.

113. C. LIPPI-BONCAMPI, *I Monti Sibillini,* Bologna, 1948, pp. 34-35.

114. In regards to this F. ALLEVI writes (op cit., p. 30, n. 14) that the excavations were undertaken "in 1921 by L. Serra and then by G. Moretti, by F. Desonay and others in 1929 and then in 1948 and finally in 1953 with the discovery of an almost certain horizontal underground passage, of an old spur, of a French coin, of a knife of ancient fabrication, etc.: in a letter to me regarding this Dr. G. Annibaldi, Superintendent of the Antiquities of the Marches, specified thusly: "the coin found on the Sibilla at a notable depth, in the tests executed by this Superintendent's office in 1953, is a double tournois of Henri II of France from the end of the 16th century, which proves, in my opinion, that the Grotto, up to a certain period, was accessible and frequented."

115. D.CECCHI, in *Il Resto del Carlino*, October 13 and 16, 1974; the article was reprinted in *La Voce* (Fossato di Vico) November 3, 1974, p.8.

116. Cf. *Il Resto del Carlino* (news of the Marches), November 18, 1974, p.8. In the same paper, after the article by Cecchi, various responses appeared, amongst which was one by Engineer A.ARRA and a response by the "Nottolini"of Macerata (Association of Speleology).

See also G.CROCETTI, *Ricerche speleologiche sui Monti Sibillini*, in *Voce delle Marche* (Fermo), August 3, 1975, p.6. Regarding the same see also the volume edited by the Santuario dell'Ambro, *San Leonardo l'Eremo dei Sibillini*, Montefortino, 1978, pp.55-57.

Finally, D. Cecchi returned to the Sibilline legends in his splendid publication *Macerata e il suo territorio- Il Paese*, Macerata, 1978, pp. 37-54.

TRANSLATORS' NOTE

Legends of the Sibilline Mountains is a small book about an obscure corner of Italy and an equally obscure backwater of world literature. And yet the themes it touches upon–amongst them, the roots of literature in popular consciousness, the intimations of Christian existentialism, the absorption of pagan traditions into Christianity–reach far and wide. Goddess worship, necromantic rites, the death of Pontius Pilate, Benvenuto Cellini, Goethe's *Faust,* Wagner's *Tannhäuser*... they all connect here in a real place of strange geological formations and magical beauty.

In this English translation our goal has been to preserve the whimsical yet serious tone of the original, which enchanted us immediately. We have to thank our cousins, Anna Maria, Claudia, and Stefania Ferri, who gave us that first copy of *Le Leggende dei Monti Sibillini* and then helped us with the translation in so many ways–including an evening in Pretare at the Festival of the Dancing Fairies.

We are grateful to Padre Giuseppe Santarelli, the author, for the pleasure his book has given us and for his kind and generous assistance. Thanks also to Padre Serafino Rafaiani and Sabina Staffinati of STAF edizioni for seeing the worth of an English version, and Catherine Sullivan and George Kulick for their help with the Latin. Finally we would never have enjoyed these legends, or the wonderful place which gave rise to them, without our many dear relatives in Abetito di Montegallo and Ascoli Piceno. We will never forget their legendary Italian hospitality.

Nathan Neel and Phoebe Leed

Nathan Neel and Phoebe Leed live in Cambridge, Massachusetts USA. Nathan Neel's maternal grandparents, Amadeo Neroni and Elia Orazi, were born in Abetito di Montegallo, Le Marche, Italy, a tiny village with a panoramic view of Monte Vettore and Monte Sibilla.